D1413657

Blaze

Dear Reader,

You can't imagine my creative giddiness when I heard about Harlequin Blaze Historical novels. I've been writing for Harlequin Blaze since #26 in the series, *Silk, Lace & Videotape*, back in 2002. And on the other hand, I've been writing sexy medievals for Harlequin Historical since my 2004 release, *The Wedding Knight*. Imagine the possibilities of a Blaze Historical novel, which for me meant incorporating the lush time period and epic backdrop of the Middle Ages with the red-hot appeal of a full-on Blaze.

If you haven't tried a historical book before, I hope you'll give *The Captive* a try. I think Gwendolyn is a medieval heroine any modern woman would root for, and Wulf is the kind of hero you could meet only in a historical novel. I think you'll agree he's worth the trip back in time!

Don't forget you can find me online at Facebook, MySpace and in the wonderfully supportive community at eHarlequin.com. And for a sneak peek at my upcoming releases from Harlequin Blaze and Harlequin Historical, don't forget to visit my Web site at www.joannerock.com.

Happy reading,

Joanne Rock

Joanne Rock

THE CAPTIVE

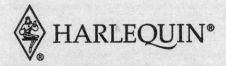

HARLEQUIN®

TORONTO • NEW YORK • LONDON
AMSTERDAM • PARiS • SYDNEY • HAMBURG
STOCKHOLM • ATHENS • TOKYO • MILAN • MADRID
PRAGUE • WARSAW • BUDAPEST • AUCKLAND

Recycling programs
for this product may
not exist in your area.

ISBN-13: 978-0-373-79538-3

THE CAPTIVE

www.eHarlequin.com

Printed in U.S.A.

ABOUT THE AUTHOR

Three-time RITA® Award nominee and Golden Heart winner Joanne Rock is the author of more than forty books for Harlequin. A fan of both medieval historicals and sexy contemporaries, she is particularly thrilled to pen her first Harlequin Blaze Historical novel, set in a medieval period. When she's not writing or spending too much time on Facebook, Joanne teaches English at the local university to share her love of the written word in all its forms. For more information, visit Joanne at www.joannerock.com.

Books by Joanne Rock

HARLEQUIN BLAZE
171—SILK CONFESSIONS
182—HIS WICKED WAYS
240—UP ALL NIGHT
256—HIDDEN OBSESSION
305—DON'T LOOK BACK
311—JUST ONE LOOK
363—A BLAZING
        LITTLE CHRISTMAS
            "His for the Holidays"
381—GETTING LUCKY
395—UP CLOSE AND PERSONAL
450—SHE THINKS HER
        EX IS SEXY...
457—ALWAYS READY
486—SLIDING INTO HOME
519—MANHUNTING
        "The Takedown"

HARLEQUIN HISTORICAL
749—THE BETROTHAL
        "Highland Handfast"
758—MY LADY'S FAVOR
769—THE LAIRD'S LADY
812—THE KNIGHT'S
        COURTSHIP
890—A KNIGHT
        MOST WICKED

For Julie Leto—I'm proud to dedicate my first
Harlequin Blaze Historical to you since
I remember so clearly the way you complimented
a historical contest entry of mine in the days
before my first sale and consequently made me
feel like a million bucks! Thank you for your
willingness to always extend a hand—not just to
me, but to so many other writers who need a lift
or advice. Cheers to you, my friend!

Prologue

Wessex, 885 AD

SOME CALLED IT THE DARK AGES, a time when the strongest men rose to power by the might of the sword. It was the era of Anglo-Saxon kings and their wars for dominance on the fertile shores of England. A young Alfred the Great ruled the Saxon kingdom of Wessex, the only British sovereign to carve out an uneasy peace with the most feared warrior race in the known world.

The Vikings.

Fierce and proud, the Norsemen came bearing swords and axes, strength and daring. Among them, one man risked more than any other, his name whispered by his enemies like that of a demon beast no one wished to conjure. He was Wulf Geirsson, heir of the ruling class, banished from his homeland for crimes shrouded in mystery. He went on to conquer lands far and wide, followed by men loyal to him alone. Who would have guessed this fiercest of Vikings would face the battle of a lifetime at the hands of a lone Saxon woman armed with no weapon save a daring to match his own?

1

"IF I HAVE TO EMBROIDER one more rose petal, I will unsheathe my eating knife and run myself through." Gwendolyn of Wessex tossed aside the linen nightgown she'd been suffering over for hours.

She despised needlework in the first place. And in the second, why bother making a night garment a work of art when her future, yet-to-be-named husband would only shred the thing off her anyway?

The women in the lesser hall stared at her in mild horror, as if they wanted nothing more from life than to stitch miniscule flower buds on a decorative garment for Gwendolyn to wear at her next wedding. As if they wanted nothing more from life than to warm a man's bed. Gwendolyn didn't even have any definite plans to wed just yet, but like all wealthy Saxon widows, she knew a union was inevitable.

The ladies who sat with her on this warm spring day were more like soulless jailors than noblewomen who embraced the happy state of widowhood as much as she did. Gwendolyn had never mourned the cruel knight who'd been foisted on her at eighteen summers, a man who had adopted the custom of keeping concubines while battling their Norse enemies. Gerald had died at the end of a Norse blade some moons ago, leaving her widowed, but waiting for the hammer to fall and her overlord to announce another marriage.

What she wouldn't give for her life to be her own. For her future to be in her hands! She'd been taught young to think for herself thanks to her parents, wealthy scholars who'd traveled the world. Their deaths on the road to Rome had devastated her. She'd spent the rest of her childhood in the custody of Richard of Alchere, an ambitious lord who'd shackled her into an advantageous marriage at the first opportunity—only to find her widowed on his doorstep two summers later.

She'd been twenty.

Now the power-hungry nobleman was so busy kissing King Alfred's royal rear, she feared what scheme the two might script for her next union.

Richard was the most powerful lord in Wessex, and he protected a key stretch of the coastline for Alfred. Alchere had been her father's neighbor before his death, after which Richard had made a fast grab for power by bringing her into his household.

While their lands may have been a neat fit against each other, Alchere's militant and unimaginative household bore no resemblance to the worldly haven her parents had ruled. Once upon a time, they had hosted scholars from all over the world to share ideas and study in their expansive library. Alchere, on the other hand, wasn't smart enough to see beyond the point of his sword. He ruled with brute force, however, and King Alfred needed military might as much as he needed scholars. Well, he needed that more, truthfully.

That military might accounted for why Gwendolyn found herself back in proud, vain Alchere's keeping

again now that her first husband had died. She'd sent a
messenger to Richard the moment she'd heard of Gerald's death in battle, knowing Alchere would gladly send
protection for her to return to him. This she did, much
as she disliked her overlord. Better in Alchere's hands
than to wait around for Gerald's family to try and keep
her inheritance by marrying her to his equally brutish
brother. She'd packed up everything she could carry and
fled the whole vicious clan.

Now, Alfred kept track of her vast dowry once again,
while Alchere kept her safe in his prison of a cold keep.
Her former in-laws would never touch her here, but
peace came at the price of her freedom.

She tipped her face into the warm sunshine filtering
in through high windows overhead; the group of widows
had been consigned to remain indoors due to fear of
raiding Danes spotted along the coast.

"Lady Gwendolyn, what will your future husband
think if your trunks are packed with naught but old
gowns sewn while you were wed to another man?"
Lady Margery currently hunted for a third spouse, so
she considered herself an expert on the matter of husbands. All the rest of the old hens looked up to her for
that reason.

Not that any of them were ancient. Margery held the
distinction of eldest at twenty-four summers. The five
women had been herded together by their king during
wartime to keep them safe since they were a valuable lot.
Each of them represented opportunities for important
political alliances upon remarriage and as such, they
required protection from the Norse raids all over the
coast. Three of the women had lost their husbands to
the bloodthirsty invaders.

"I do not even have a marriage contracted," Gwendolyn pointed out for the tenth time in a fortnight. She'd put forth a great deal of effort to keep it that way since the idea of another marriage made her blood run cold. "And if I did, he would surely ignore my bridal clothes in the rush to the marriage bed anyhow. Why would any man care about the needlework on a lady's nightgown when their only interest is ripping a woman's garb from her body?"

She shivered with distaste. Gerald had handled her roughly those first few months of their marriage. Later, when he'd gone back to his concubines, he'd visited her less often, but his touch had remained abhorrent. Painful. Gwendolyn could not understand why some women spoke of marital pleasures with blushes and giggles. She'd found no tenderness in her husband's bed.

"Perhaps," Lady Margery began, peering over the tapestry she embroidered along with the others, "that is why Lord Richard finds it such a difficult challenge to obtain a good marriage for you. The poor man does not think you will be able to behave with any sort of decorum for the summer let alone a whole year."

Gwendolyn closed her eyes to let the inciting comment wash over her rather than box the woman's ears the way Margery fully deserved.

Once the other women stifled their giggles, Gwen shot to her feet and circled the benches they'd drawn up next to each other, wishing she could run on the fresh green grasses outside rather than pace a musty old hall. The lack of activity combined with the need to keep a civil tongue would make her sheep-brained in no time.

"Lord Richard is not finding it *difficult* to contract my marriage." Her youth and her wealth made her a sought-after bride, if nothing else. She did not deceive herself that men wanted her for her submissive manner or extravagant beauty. The years with Gerald had only made her more unwilling to cater to any man. "I have been actively bartering with Alchere for more time to consider the candidates so I might weigh in on his decision for my next spouse."

At least, that was the version of events she preferred. And it contained some truth. But Margery put down the corner of a small tapestry she worked on to better lift her snooty nose in the air.

"Lady Gwendolyn, we all know the earl asked you to remain out of trouble for a full year before he'd ever consider letting you choose a husband for yourself." Margery's gaze returned to the patch of needlework where she stitched the outline of a pasty-faced maiden. "He only offered such a boon since he is certain you will never fulfill your end. We all know you'll be wed to someone, whether you will it or nay, before next harvest."

Ah, another nip to Gwen's pride. Gwendolyn had a bit of a reputation for mischief-making, and she'd never been able to resist an opportunity to tweak her overlord's arrogant nose. Of course, she'd lived in Alchere's awful stronghold for far more years than these widows who came and went under his all-mighty protection, so she knew how wretched he could be. His tempers were notorious and his dictates ranged from unfair to downright evil. He'd even forced her to burn the books that she'd inherited from her father's household so that she would not grow "too self-important with knowledge."

The book burning had nearly killed her. Could she help it if during her youth she took what revenge she could by occasionally adorning his ugly mug with beauty paints while he slept off too much drink? Or tucked the bones he discarded onto the great hall floor inside his boots so the castle hounds gnawed him mercilessly?

None of the other women understood her long and frustrating relationship with Alchere, however. They only saw that she baited the man wherever possible. So a retort rose quickly to Gwen's tongue to set Margery straight on the matter of Alchere, but it was cut off by the abrupt opening of the hall's doors from the other side.

A page of no more than eight or nine summers burst through the entrance, his eyes wide.

"Ladies, you must hasten to the keep." He did not bother with courtesy, but began grabbing their embroidery to carry away. He spilled a basket of threads and stepped on the corner of a half-finished tapestry. "The Norsemen's boats make their way close to shore."

Gwendolyn forgot all about her quarrel with Margery and the soul-smothering boredom of the women's conversations about husbands. She understood the danger the enemy presented. Their raids had cost many lives, much gold and countless maidens' innocence. These invading warriors were brutes that had terrorized lands far and wide. The only part of England where they did not have a toehold was Wessex, as King Alfred had made a pact to keep them away.

But when you bargained with devils, who was to say they would honor it? Only a fool wouldn't know fear.

"Hurry," the young page implored, his wide, dark eyes frightened. "The boats came from the north where the view is thick with trees. The watch did not see—"

"Go," she ordered him, pointing toward the doors where the other women fled in a flurry of colorful skirts. "I must retrieve something from my chamber."

She lurched toward the door, wanting to gather up

the few belongings that were truly hers—belongings greedy Alchere did not know about. She'd managed to save one of her father's books from the lord's burning frenzy and she would not see that prized possession hacked to pieces by pillaging Danes.

The boy tugged on her sleeve. "There is no time. I was told to have all the women in the keep at once. They will lock you in to ensure your safety."

As if anywhere was safe when the Norse terror came. These Danes could sniff out riches from many leagues distant, and that surely included a barricaded keep full of heiresses. Gwendolyn guessed she would be safer on the walls with an armed knight before her than stashed away with all the other lucrative possessions. Still, right now all she cared about was her father's journal. One last tie to her parents that no man would pry from her fingers.

"You have done your duty," she told the page, walking with him to the door. But as they reached the timber corridor that opened onto the courtyard, she pried his fingers from her wrist. "You may say I refused to go with you, but unless you plan to drag me by force, I will not retreat just yet."

The boy appeared ready to argue, his brows knitted in a fierce frown. But then he shrugged helplessly and ran off, leaving her unattended. Alchere would be in a fury if he learned of it. And didn't that suit her just fine? For all she knew, her king and overlord could start bartering off wealthy widows as part of their ongoing bargain with the Danes to keep them away. Perhaps that was Alchere's purpose in gathering the women together—not to keep them safe, but to use them as bribes to the enemy. Gwendolyn had no intention of making herself available for a political alliance with a bloodthirsty heathen.

Lifting her skirts, she raced through the gallery above the great hall and found her chamber. Retrieving the journal swiftly, she tucked the hide-bound book into her garter that held her stocking and retied the knot to secure it. Then, peering about the small chamber that had been hers since childhood, she sought anything else that she wanted to bring. Heart racing, she scooped up a handful of rings and tucked them into a small pouch that hung from her girdle. On her way out the door, as a last moment thought, she plucked her first marriage veil from where it dangled off a flag post that held her family's old banner.

Pushing it over the plaits wound about her head, Gwendolyn knew the veil counted as the most costly item in her wardrobe. The circlet incorporated price-less jewels from both sides of her family and boasted metalwork from the finest goldsmith in Wessex. If the keep was overrun today, she'd rather have items of value with her than sitting here unprotected.

Fleeing from her chamber like a thief with stolen goods, she was headed for the stairs down to the court-yard when a horn and shouts nearby caught her by surprise.

Undeniable curiosity warred with good sense.

Had the invaders arrived? Was battle imminent? She caught a whiff of the sea breeze rolling in off the water and smelled change on the wind. She'd sensed it once before—that day her parents left her for their trip to Rome, she'd somehow known despite their assurances that her life would never be the same. She had that same tickle along her senses now and wanted to confront her fate rather than hide from it. If she went out there—up to the castle walls right now—maybe she would know what was coming before it happened. Maybe she could make a difference by alerting Richard to...

She knew not what exactly, but that desire to affect her future drew her feet toward the stone steps that led up to the partition over the courtyard. Quietly. Discreetly. She was adept at climbing all over the keep, quick as a cat, to spy on Alchere. Of course, she'd been more of an intrepid scout at fourteen years old, back when she'd hung from the rafters to drop a fat, furry spider into Alchere's ale after the book burning. She had hoped the creature would be poisonous, but no such luck.

Now, she dashed up to the walls, filled with the hopefulness of her daring. The more she thought about it, the more certain she became that Alchere would bargain away his lucrative widows before he let the Danes overrun the keep. The raiders could take the women and demand their inheritance and holdings from King Alfred. Alfred would pay the way he'd always done in the past to keep peace. How many treaties had he negotiated with these knaves already?

Gwendolyn would have none of it. She did not even want a Saxon husband to rule her, but a Dane? Just the thought of it had her trembling in her slippers. If her husband's touch had hurt her, what would it be like to share a bed with a man twice his size? Never. She would simply steal away to the stables when no one was looking. She could hire a protector to take her somewhere far away. To Rome, perhaps. Or any one of the other places her father spoke of with such fondness...

But right now, she needed to see what was really happening outside the keep to form her plan. As she climbed higher toward the ramparts, Gwendolyn's pouch of rings swung against her leg. The scent of the sea wafted toward her along with smoke from the forgery and the metallic *ting* of the blacksmith's arts. The smells of weaponry and battle.

Creeping quietly to the small tower parapet where no guard sat watch, Gwendolyn suppressed a shiver. From the coming danger presented by the Danes? Or the potential for greater dangers outside these walls? Leaving Alchere's protection could invite pursuit by her in-laws if they ever found out. They had been furious to lose their lucrative heiress when Gerald died, but Alchere insisted they were not entitled to keep her lands and wealth when their union had not produced an heir.

Nervousness churned her stomach. One thing was certain, however. The boats pulling up to the shore beneath the outer walls were unlike anything Gwendolyn had seen before.

Low and sleek, the arriving Norse ships were simple affairs packed with oars and men. Carved wooden figureheads peered proudly from the front of each ship, the fierce angle of the heads marking them as dragons or some other fantastical creature even from this distance. Between Gwendolyn and the oncoming ships—twenty, perhaps—the courtyard below hummed with activity. Warriors hauled weaponry to the walls from storerooms in the keep. Quivers full of arrows appeared from the protective nooks where they were normally kept to keep their feathers crisp. Cauldrons had been set over a bonfire, no doubt boiling some substance to be dumped upon anyone foolish enough to climb the fortifications.

Would it be enough to keep the marauders away?

Gwendolyn sensed the fear in the air. Alchere had boasted enough about his impregnable keep, but he had not fought the scourge of the north, the Norsemen who burned abbeys after raiding the relics and ravaging the women.

The swift boats were landing even now, gliding silently onto the beach all around. Why weren't Alchere's men firing on them? Had she been correct to assume they would give these raiders anything they asked to keep them at bay? From up here, she could see no way out of the keep, let alone a clear path to travel if she could reach the stable and secure a horse. Crouching low on her way to the farthest corner nook, she avoided notice from Alchere's men who congregated on the southern facade, closest to where the Danes gathered. She leaned out over the wall on a vacant section of the ramparts to see the invaders for herself.

The Norsemen were barbaric-looking. Large men, their stony visages reflected their warlike disposition. Their leather braies stretched over muscular thighs, while their light tunics snapped in the breeze against massive chests. This race that had conquered half of Britain was every bit as fearsome as she'd imagined.

Holding down her veils to keep them from flapping in the wind, she tried to staunch the panic rising up in her throat. She could not afford to be taken by these men. Not as a pawn in some misguided bartering by Alchere, and not as a battle prize by marauding brutes. These men would hurt her as Gerald had hurt her.

Or worse.

Panic bloomed in her belly. She spied her overlord riding out to meet the assembled throng of warriors. Wasn't that the action of a man prepared to negotiate peace instead of fight for it?

By God, she would not serve as a peace offering to some lustful Dane.

Backing away from the edge of the wall, heart

hammering her chest, she thought about where to hide. Bits of stone broke beneath her feet and skittered down the wall. Nowhere was safe. She needed to—

Her veil caught on the rocks in the wind, the fine silk snagging. Hands shaking, she reached to untwine it. She'd been foolish to wear it. She should have tied it about her waist, but it had not occurred to her she might really need to leave—

"Ow!" She winced as she yanked her hair in her haste and still did not free the veil. Stepping closer to the edge of the wall, she lifted the fabric straight up to dislodge the snag. Just as the material came loose, a few rocks gave way beneath her feet.

Her foot slipped. She gasped, her arms wheeling round, but finding naught but air to steady herself. In one gut-wrenching moment of clarity, she knew she would fall and break her neck on the rocks below.

But at the last moment, strong arms belted about her waist, snatching her back from the edge as she pitched forward.

Impossible. A miracle! Her brain could not comprehend what happened as limbs thick as tree trunks wrapped about her and hauled backward on her rump, dragging her to safety on the parapet wall.

Relief burst through her like giddy laughter. She'd been saved from certain death.

Turning toward her savior, her veil ripped and hanging limply to one side, she discovered a sight that led her to wish she'd flung herself to the beach below. Because the man who had saved her was no proud Saxon warrior, but the most terrifying enemy she could imagine.

She'd been rescued by a Viking.

2

A SCREAM ROSE TO HER LIPS.

Somehow, with the same lightning-fast reflexes that had saved her from falling off the wall, the invader guessed her intent and clapped a mighty hand over her mouth to stifle it.

"Quiet." Speaking a halting Saxon tongue, he growled the word low into her ear as he tugged her back against his chest and drew her to her feet in front of him. "You do not want your men to fire upon you in their haste to kill me, do you?"

Her heart pounded so hard she felt dizzy and light-headed with it. She would have fallen to her knees if not for one thick arm pressed to her waist and the other pinning her shoulders. Her impressions of him were disjointed, it had all happened so fast. He was big even for a barbarian. Broad in the chest, thick in the arms. But his hair was dark like a Saxon's. It was his size and blue eyes that marked him for a Dane. That and his absurd manner of dress—the cross-gartered braies and the cut of the heavy fur cloak that swung carelessly down his back.

He moved with her now, this nameless wall of

muscle, pushing her toward the most remote stretch of the parapets.

Unbidden, her hands reached to pull his fingers off her mouth. She dragged her feet and scratched him, desperate to be free. He would take her captive. Abuse her. Pass her along to his men. Her belly clenched and she thought she would be sick.

"Be still," he commanded softly, swinging one leg over the castle wall as if he would kill them both by jumping to the beach. However, he paid no heed to her efforts to free herself. She would have never guessed he even noticed them if not for the quiet order in her ear.

Now, he lifted her in his arms to cradle her like a child while he clambered down a crumbled staircase that led to an outer bailey. She'd forgotten this passage off the wall even existed, but then it had been in disrepair ever since she'd arrived here as a girl. The Dane must be mad to tread his heavy foot upon such faulty stonework.

Praying fervently someone would notice them before he escaped the keep all together, Gwendolyn rubbed the back of her head along his arm while he climbed, hoping she could free some of her veil to float in the breeze like a silken flag. Perhaps the jewels and the color would catch someone's attention as they descended onto the ground floor of the castle.

When that did not work, she twisted her head hard to one side. Escaping his confining hand, she screamed. Far better to risk one of Alchere's archers shooting her in the leg than to submit peacefully to a heathen who would brutalize her.

"Son of a swine!" she shouted, her mind blank of better insults in the face of her fear. "Rot in Hades, you sheep-loving maggot!"

Too soon, he replaced his hand over her mouth and bent low to speak in her ear.

"There is no one." The heavy accent of his homeland made his words difficult to distinguish even though he spoke a Saxon language for her sake. "The lord of the keep is too busy flexing his might on the southern side to spare a man for the north. He is a strong fighter and a stupid tactician."

Was it true?

Sweet, merciful heaven, it must be. How else would this iron-fisted demon be able to breach the fortifications? Why did no one come when she'd called? The heathen moved quiet as a cat, even with her in his arms. Panic bubbled higher.

This time, she bit his hand to free her mouth.

"Danes within the walls!" she shrieked, her sole outburst before he wrenched her tighter, his fingers digging into her cheek as he clamped her lips once again. She tasted his blood on her tongue, and this time she could not move.

As he neared a small gate intended for wood carts and other supplies, Gwendolyn realized the watchtower was empty and other Danes were slipping in and out the entrance, shouldering expensive pieces of the chapel altar and heavy chests that spilled coins on the courtyard stones.

The heathen and his men robbed Alchere blind while her overlord thought he conducted negotiations with them.

And just like her worst fear, she would be part of the war spoils. A captive to the most fearsome man she'd ever seen.

WULF GEIRSSON HAD HARDLY thought anything could tempt him on the raid of a Wessex stronghold held by one of King Alfred's strongest knights. He didn't need more riches, after all. As the most successful Viking raider to sail on the coast of Britain, he had more wealth than he'd ever dreamed. He hadn't even organized the attack on this keep today, but when his small band of men had spied the troop of Danes congregating on a nearby shore to plot the battle the night before, he hadn't been able to resist the opportunity to thieve the raid from under their noses. He'd planned to simply flaunt his skill before his enemies and make off with the biggest prizes simply because he *could,* not because the riches tempted him.

But, enjoying the feel of the woman in his arms, he realized he could not have been more wrong. He'd been tempted when he'd least expected it.

The sweetly scented captive fighting tooth and nail against his hold was an unexpected boon. When he'd spied the audacious Saxon beauty climbing up to look out over the castle walls in the hour before battle, he'd been struck first by her dark, exotic look. Brown locks flowed in a glossy stream down her back, dark eyes lit with glints of gold as she narrowed them in the sunlight. Assessing the enemy?

He did not know what she'd sought on the ramparts when all the other women were surely locked safely in the castle's innermost sanctum. This maid alone had not hidden in the face of a Norse raid, and that snagged his attention more thoroughly than any surface beauty. When was the last time he'd found a female so brazen? Maids who cowered throughout a raid held no appeal. He did not brutalize women.

But fire and spirit in a female? This intrigued him. He'd made up his mind he wanted her—that he would take her—even before she'd nearly fallen off the parapet.

The fact that he had surely saved her pretty neck only made him more certain he'd been destined to have her.

Now, he sprinted away from the keep with the woman in his arms, ready to meet his men and depart before Alchere learned they'd been there. Before the other Danes who led the invading party discovered his men had taken their spoils while they wasted time with talk down on the beach.

"Only a little farther," he assured the woman, feeling her shaking against him. Of course, she would be frightened now, no matter how bold she'd appeared earlier. "Our boats are hidden nearby, just through these trees."

He could have set her on her feet, but he suspected she would not move quickly enough for his liking. He did, however, remove his hand from her mouth so that he could balance her weight more evenly in his arms.

"A curse upon you!" she screamed immediately, nearly deafening him as he reached the longship already packed with three quarters of his men. "You rank and craven boar! Reeking devil's spawn!"

"By Thor's beard, Wulf, can you not gag her?"

Wulf's cousin, Erik, waited in the bow of the boat, his gaze darting in the direction of the other invaders on the shore close to Alchere's keep.

"A lone, shrieking woman will hardly draw notice during a Norse raid." In his experience, there were generally a handful of females in every town who screeched from the moment the longships were spotted until the last boat had taken its leave.

Wading through the shallows to the ship, Wulf debated handing her over to Erik while he boarded. There was no choice, really. If not for Wulf's iron grip on her,

the writhing maid would have flung herself into the
sea or cracked her skull on the side of the ship in the
attempt, so settling her on the deck without someone
restraining her was not an option. Still, the thought of
Erik's hands on the captive sent a surge of possessiveness through him.

Resettling her in his arms, he was able to keep her
cradled while replacing a hand over her mouth. Her
screeching halted at the same time he paused at the side
of the ship.

She looked less like a haughty noblewoman and more
like a trapped animal. Trembling all over, her eyes wide
with fright, she felt cold to the touch even though sweat
beaded along her brow.

Strands of dark hair and golden ribbons trailed over
her cheek, everything askew from her struggle. Pink
color flamed along her creamy cheeks and neck. She
weighed nothing at all, her skirts and cloak accounting
for most of the bulk in his arms. But her strong will
was evident in the way her elbow still rammed his chest
and her hips twisted for freedom despite his superior
strength. Many women fainted at the sight of a marauding army.

Not this one.

He could already imagine the feel of her surrender
beneath him. And it would not be the momentary satisfaction he normally took from lying with a woman.
A bold wench who climbed castle walls to look out on
the battlefield would present a challenge that appealed
to the tactician in him. He would enjoy this.

"We will not be at sea for long," he confided, his
words soft for her ears alone. Erik would think he'd lost
his wits to comfort a captive. Indeed, he could not say
for certain why he bothered. But something about the

woman had enthralled him from the first. "This ship
is built for speed and can take us where we are going
quickly."

"Hand her over, Wulf," Erik bit out through gritted
teeth. "We should make haste before Harold finds out
his spoils have been stolen out from under his men."

Cursing the need to let anyone save him touch her,
Wulf deposited the woman in Erik's arms while he lifted
himself out of the surf and into the ship. Seawater clung
to his braies, the cooling effect welcome after the way
the nameless Saxon lass had set fire to him.

She screamed more insults about their mothers,
their gods and their resemblance to various animals in
the moments when no one had her mouth covered, but
Wulf's men were too well trained to comment on his
unwillingness to gag her. The Danes who sailed with
him were an elite force of men who'd worked together
ever since he'd been old enough to command his own
ship. These were the men who'd remained loyal to him
when he'd been driven from his homeland by Harold
Haaraldson.

Harold held Wulf responsible for his sister's death.
Truth be told, Wulf blamed himself, so he'd never protested the exile. But after a year of seafaring and raiding, never pausing in one place more than a week or
two, Wulf knew he would have to face Harold's wrath
one day. Perhaps that had been part of the reason he'd
tweaked the Danish king's pride today by stealing
away the wealth from his raid. Now a confrontation
was inevitable.

"Give her to me," Wulf commanded, unwilling to
tie the lady to the ship and hoping he could subdue her
instead. He would not allow her to jump overboard while

they were out to sea. One woman's death on his hands was enough.

"Get off me, you toad-licking lout!" the Saxon shouted, lunging toward the water as Erik passed her to him.

Both men were forced to reposition their footing, rocking the boat.

"She is trouble," Erik warned. "And since when do we take captives?" He'd raised his voice over the woman's shouts for help and curses upon the Danes.

A few of the men at the oars chuckled appreciatively as her oaths turned more colorful, involving swines' asses and sheep dung. Though how one could sensibly follow the other, he was not certain.

"I will have this one." He made the rules before the raid. Typically, they did not take prisoners without planning well for them in advance. They traveled leaner than most Vikings, so they could not provide for captives often. "Drop the oars in."

By now all the men had returned. No head count was needed since every man had a seat at the oars save him. He took a turn to relieve Erik on longer journeys, but not this one. Not when he was eager to reach land with the woman. Her breasts rose and fell rapidly from her efforts, drawing his eye to linger on her shapely form.

With nary a splash, the ship slid from the shore and the woman made a keening cry.

"Curses will rain down upon you for this, heathens," she warned all the men in the boat.

They paid her no heed, steering the craft away from the Wessex keep, out of the reach of Harold Haaraldson. His enemy would be furious when he realized he'd been thwarted in this raid.

Richard of Alchere, the captive's overlord, would also

be greedy for revenge. Would he know to seek Wulf? Or would he think his riches rested with Haaraldson? Nay, Alchere was not the smartest tactician, but the dead watchmen on the keep's northern gate would tell the story of Wulf's stealthy scheme. Wulf did not have much time before they would seek him.

Alchere would no doubt seek *her,* as well.

She was a prize fit for a lord, but he could not imagine she was Alchere's wife. Wulf found the idea repugnant. She belonged to no one but him from this day forward.

He peered down at her now quieting in his arms though the fury had not left her eyes. Perhaps she had decided to save her strength for a future fight. She must know it would do her no good to gain her freedom only to find herself in the middle of an ocean.

She did not turn green from the motion of the hull slicing through the waves, the way he'd seen some men do. The Saxon mistress had at least some small affinity for the sea. A fortunate thing for a woman who would belong to a seafaring man.

"You have a plan for her now?" Erik asked from his spot at the oars.

The longship held places for twelve oarsmen on each side. This close to the coast, they did not raise the lone sail, preferring to maneuver quickly up the small rivers and estuaries off the sea.

"We'll separate since Harold will be searching for me. You continue with the rest of the men west. We will lay low for a few days until Haaraldson's temper passes." A strand of the maid's silken hair blew against his neck, a sweetly seductive caress.

"Assuming it ever passes. And what of Alchere? He will surely search for the woman." This time Erik turned and he missed the downbeat of the rowing altogether. "You bring the wrath of too many at once—"

"Nay. We are faster because we are fewer. If other Danes see you, they will not see *her* because she will be with me." The best part of the plan was that he would have her alone. Perhaps she would not fight so hard when she saw there was no one to contend with but him. "There is an abandoned church ruin in a cove around a small bend ahead. Drop me there with the woman while you take the men farther up the coast for a few days' rest. 'Tis all I need to slake a sudden thirst, and when I finish, I will reward the men's idle time with a voyage farther west."

It was a time-honored bribe to seafaring men. The promise of sailing uncharted waters enticed them faster than gold. Besides, they would need to stay well out of Haaroldson's grasp for a few weeks before they commenced raiding this stretch of shore again.

On his lap, the woman tipped her chin into the spray of the water, some of the tension easing from her shoulders. She had not looked toward him once since they left the shore, her gaze trained on the land as they rowed hard along the coast. He wanted to say something to reassure her, but to do so in front of his men would not be wise. They had been dutiful enough to indulge this fancy of his. They did not need to suffer any more of his personal affair.

"They will come looking for you," Erik assured him.

"They will not find me." He would make sure he had time to explore the soft curves of the creature in his arms first. Her every twitch and wriggle imprinted knowledge of her body in his brain, making him all the more hungry to have her.

"Your luck will run out, especially if you insist on besting Harold in raids. He will not rest until he has the revenge he's sought all year." Erik spoke a naked truth that wrenched him from his thoughts about the dark-haired captive.

A familiar storm brewed within him, at odds with the clear day. A year at sea had not made the clouds of the past dissipate.

It was true that Hedra Haaraldson—Harold's sister—had taken her life because of Wulf.

"Hard to shore," Wulf commanded, earning a grunt from one of his men and a rapid string of oaths from Erik.

He would not think of Hedra. Losing himself between the thighs of the vixen in his arms would banish all other thoughts from his head.

"We have not reached the lodging you wanted." Despite obvious frustration, Erik pulled his oar up from the water so the rowers on the other side of the ship could steer the craft toward land.

"No. We can travel the rest of the way on foot. The fresh air will be more welcome than speaking of a past I cannot change." He did not think the old ruins he recalled could be far off. But he could live off the land if necessary.

Besides, the thunder brewing in his head needed release. And the willful maiden who fumed silently in his arms seemed an obvious companion to ride out the storm.

IN THEIR TIME AT SEA, no man spared her a glance save the leader. Wulf, the other man had called him.

Of course, Gwendolyn thought, one of the stony-faced oarsmen might have stolen a glance her way while her gaze had been tipped out to sea. But their backs had been to her as they rowed the ship, and she'd never *felt* an untoward stare from anyone except the brooding Norseman who held her fast against his hard-muscled chest.

When he'd given the order to head toward shore, she'd sensed the dissension between him and the only other man who'd spoken on the voyage. It seemed her captor had earned the enmity of more than just her overlord. Someone named Harold would be searching for him.

And heaven help him if her in-laws ever found out she'd been taken. They hated the Danes enough without knowing their lost prize had come under the control of the race of men who'd killed their precious Gerald. They would stake their claim to her—and her fortune that King Alfred controlled until her next marriage—with all haste.

All of which should have cheered her. It meant she would not be ruled by this Dane for long. But it only served to hammer home that her life would never be her own. "Rescue" by any of those parties only meant that someone else would have power over her life.

Now, as they navigated around rocks and driftwood into a quiet cove, Gwendolyn tamped down her fears and wondered what happened next. Had she been taken to the middle of nowhere only to be abused by a ship full of marauders?

She'd dismissed the niggling fear dozens of time during the trip since a ship full of invaders would have surely been much happier to ravage a whole village full of women. And the leader had made it sound as if he would be alone with her.

By the saints.

The thought would terrify any woman. But she was

not a maid ignorant of the ways of men. She knew that a man's touch could bring wrenching pain. And that had been in the bed of her *husband*. What would it be like with a heathen with no legal tie to her?

While the oars lifted from the water, bringing the warship to a crawl and then a halt mere feet from land, the Norseman gave some command to his men. He spoke in the quick, harsh language of the Danes that bore some small resemblance to her Saxon tongue, but not enough for her to comprehend. She'd understood snippets of what he'd said back on the boat, but he'd been speaking more slowly then. Now, she guessed he said something about his thanks and a meeting, but nothing that gave her any clearer idea what he had in mind here.

Then, he stood and allowed her to do the same, apparently trusting her not to pitch herself overboard now that he'd taken her too far from home to swim back. She debated leaping into the sea anyhow, but with a whole ship full of men at the oars, she could hardly outpace them.

"We depart," he announced in his accented version of her language, then waited.

"I do not understand." She shook her head, confused. They had not reached a keep or even an encampment.

"You and I are remaining here." He gestured to the sandy cliffs that rose up from the water and ended in patches of thicket and trees. "I will help you ashore."

"No." She edged back, pressing herself against the carved dragonhead at the ship's bow. The beast's fierce aspect seemed a fitting figurehead for the sword-wielding heathens who manned the craft.

He frowned, his thick, dark eyebrows swooping low over azure blue eyes. "How are you called, lady?"

Did he truly not guess her name? Indeed, she'd hoped

that he had known of her identity prior to arrival at her keep. If he did not know of her and her wealth as an heiress, what reason could he possibly have for taking her? He'd risked his life and his men's by entering Alchere's stronghold.

"I am Gwendolyn of Wessex."

"Very well, Gwendolyn of Wessex, if you will not come willingly, I will be forced to carry you again. I would point out there is no sense screaming since this stretch of your coast is uninhabited."

"You're serious."

He intended for her to disembark here, in the middle of nowhere. He would allow her to choose whether she wished to be toted around like a bundle of hay by him again, or else swim like a dog through waist-high water.

Her father's journal—still tied to her thigh—could be ruined. It had a leather sleeve of sorts, but she did not trust it to keep the water out of the pages. She wasn't sure why the journal mattered now when she needed to think of her own neck, but she had so little that was hers alone. As a woman, all the properties and wealth she'd inherited would never really belong to her. They went to her husband. Or the sons she might one day bear.

"I do not wish to depart." She put the notion out there, hoping perhaps his argumentative friend would use it as a reason to stand up for her. The other man had not seemed pleased that Wulf had taken her.

Would the man protect her?

She braved a look in that warrior's direction, but the man kept his attention on his oars as did the whole cursed ship full of Danes. Was there not a single chivalrous soul among them? Not to mention a nosy one?

While her head was turned, the Norse leader jumped

overboard with a splash. On him, the water did not rise much higher than his knees. And once he had his footing, he reached back for her. He swooped close and, like a hawk plucks a field mouse from the ground, he lifted her high in his arms and carried her toward the shore.

She yelped and flailed in his grasp only a moment before his grip tightened. Fear made her lightheaded.

"Put me down, you overgrown lout." She could scarcely move once he determined it necessary to hold her tight. "I cannot breathe."

"Talking requires breath," he assured her, striding through the water and up onto the sandy shore.

He could have easily set her on her feet then. She would not soak her shoes now that they hit land. But the man built like an oak tree continued to hold her fast, his hands making themselves more familiar with her body than even her husband's had as the Dane's fingers cupped the side of her breast beneath one arm.

Heaven knew her spouse had only been interested in the most rudimentary of rutting, so he had not bothered to touch her anywhere but the most crucial of places. And wasn't that an absurd thought to have now of all times? Panic must be causing her brain to think strange things.

"Honestly, I can walk," she protested, unsettled as much by being left alone on the beach with the Viking leader as she was by her realization that she'd just compared her captor to her husband.

Not that it was completely off target.

She'd been at the utter mercy of each. She did not dare an escape attempt until she knew there was somewhere to go. She did not think for a moment she could outrun the foreigner. And she could not lose him in broad daylight. Especially not when he could still call back his friends in the longship.

"We can move faster this way. I will lower you when we reach the top of the rise."

She followed his blue gaze to the hilltop covered in low trees and recalled the steep incline she'd seen from the ship. Dear Lord, the man had already charged up half of it. Leaving her with the rest of his climb to consider her next move as he held her fast to his chest.

"I can pay you to leave me alone," she realized suddenly. If he had not known her identity, he could not know how much she was worth. "I am an heiress. My overlord will pay well for my safe return. You can barter with him the way your ruler bargains with King Alfred for peace in Wessex."

"I have enough riches." His thighs brushed her rump as he climbed, his strides long to climb the hill.

"No man believes that." Although, now that she thought about it, her father had believed it. He had inherited such extensive lands from his father that just managing them well took much of his time. He'd never wished to acquire more. But since his death, she'd never met another soul—male or female—who thought that way.

"I will accept no price for you." He glanced down at her then and his gaze stirred a prickle of warning along her skin. Her flesh fairly hummed with it.

Acute awareness traveled through her, a sudden hot warning that she must free herself from his grasp. There was too much intimacy about it. He held her so closely she could feel the warmth of his skin emanating through his tunic. And where his thighs brushed her rump, she could feel the dampness of his braies from his dive into the sea. His tunic and skin both held a scent of some spicy herb he must use to wash. Bergamot or perhaps it was some plant native to his region.

"Release me," she demanded, arching away from him.

"Almost." He climbed on, heedless of her struggle. "There is another rise after the first."

She'd only succeeded in twisting the hem of her gown. A cool breeze fluttered up beneath it, teasing her legs and exposing her calves. Her cheeks burned and she counseled patience. She would simply wait until he set her down. For now, however, she distracted him by asking a question that occurred to her.

"You know my name, but I do not know yours." She'd heard him called Wulf, of course, but what of a family name?

"Wulf Geirsson." He turned his head to look upon her and she remembered how close they were. His straight blade of a nose hovered less than a hand's span away. She watched his hard, sculpted mouth form the unusual name, the primitive sound bringing to mind the fierce beast that shared it.

"Why did you take only me, Wulf Geirsson?"

She feared the answer, yet it had to be asked. And she might never feel so bold with him as she did right now, absorbing the beat of his heart along the side of her chest. A man would not treat her violently after ensuring she did not get her shoes wet while disembarking, would he?

His foot slid in the sandy cliff face, but she never worried he would drop her. She could not imagine a warrior any stronger or more capable than this one. Righting his feet, he chose a more zagging path for the end of the climb.

"I did not intend to take you at first. But I have been

forced to roam the sea all year long, with naught but raiding to relieve the boredom."

"You have tired of defiling churches." She did not hide the bite in her tone. She'd seen his men hefting the altarpiece to Alchere's ornate chapel into their longship. But she could not see what his answer had to do with his reasons for taking her. Fear and frustration made her careless with her words.

"I do not defile churches. I merely tire of the endless raiding. When I spied you on the battlements of the keep, I knew I would pursue something besides gold or relics worth a fortune I do not need."

"Have you found your conscience then?" Perhaps he would repent. But the dark look that turned his eyes from azure to sea-blue did not appear full of remorse for his deeds. If anything, he suddenly had the appearance of a man who wished to devour her whole.

She gulped. Why had she not learned to keep her comments to herself?

"Instead of gold, I have decided to pursue pleasure. And the first pleasure on my list is you."

3

"PUT ME DOWN." GWENDOLYN'S icy words suggested she had not appreciated his plan where she was concerned.

Wulf did not break his stride.

"On the other side of the tree line—"

"Put me down!" Her high, thready voice hit an odd note as her heartbeat throbbed in a blue vein at her neck.

He could also feel the dizzying pace of the pulse in that tender curve just below her breast where he cradled her. He seemed to have sent her into a full-blown panic.

Could she be so naive? What else would he take her for if not the wealth he could barter for her return?

Reaching the top of the cliff, he stopped and put her down. No sooner had her feet hit the ground than she tore off ahead of him, as fast as her shorter legs and long, heavy skirts would allow.

As luck would have it, she ran in the direction of the ruins he sought anyhow. But she ran with such heedless abandon, branches snapped and tore at her clothing, surely scratching the delicate skin beneath. Foolish woman.

He gave chase, moving with stealth so he did not scare her unnecessarily. If she fell from a high ledge, all of his effort in taking her would be for naught. He almost had her in his grasp when she stepped on a low patch of earth and tumbled.

"Oh!" Her cry of distress was genuine, but her injury could not have been serious. She sprawled in pine needles and long dead leaves, but then scrambled up again, back on her feet to limp away.

"It is not enough you nearly fell from the ramparts today? Must you throw yourself from the cliffs, as well?"

He caught her easily, locking an arm about her waist. Perhaps, now that she was hurt, she would see the wisdom in following where he led. Briefly, he debated investigating the extent of her injuries since the idea of peeling up her skirts held considerable appeal. But he sensed the fight had not gone out of her yet.

"Where are you taking me?" She winced with the first few halting steps, so he bore a bit more of her weight. "If you sought no more than a moment's pleasure, you could have taken it on the beach."

"Perhaps I seek more than a moment."

"Maybe a moment is all you can afford since I am a prisoner of great worth. My overlord will seek me before he hunts for the altarpiece you stole. We do not have much time." She peered over her shoulder as if she half expected a rescue to come riding up the cliffs at any moment.

It seemed the woman was no stranger to spinning lies convincingly. A less experienced warrior might have believed her.

"Are you wed to Alchere?" That was the only reason he could imagine the Saxon overlord mounting a search party immediately. Otherwise, the only thing driving him would be pride. And while that would no doubt bring him in search of Gwendolyn soon enough, it would not draw him out of his protected keep while Harold Haaraldson remained at his walls.

Wulf had a day or two here with her at least before he'd need to secure her better.

"Of course not." Her lip curled in distaste. "Alchere is an arrogant pig—"

She bit off the words with a quick glance to his face. Worried. Considering. Wulf laughed at the transparent thoughts in her expressive face because midway through the passionate assertion, she seemed to realize it might have helped her cause to claim marriage to him.

"Too late, Gwen." Wulf lifted her gently over a rotten log, the damp of spring making the ground give under their feet. "I would not have believed you anyhow. The Danes already know your king has entrusted Alchere with several high-born widows of political importance to the kingdom. I imagine if Alchere was ever given permission to choose one of his wards for himself, he would not pick the most imprudent one of the lot."

"How dare you—"

"He would also not choose a woman who did not obey him implicitly," he continued, ignoring her obvious desire to argue. "If you were his wife, he would have ensured you were locked in his bedchamber with a guard at the door before a raid."

He paused at a sound in the trees, quickly drawing Gwendolyn close and putting his hand over her mouth to staunch any noise. They had not been followed from the beach, but what if they'd strayed close a nobleman's land? He would never be mistaken for a Saxon, even at a distance.

In that moment of stillness and silence, he peered down at his captive. A fresh cut marred her cheek from her run through the trees to escape. The veil she'd torn on a rock back on the parapet now had even more holes in the delicate material. But above the constraining weight of his hands, her eyes peered at him with dark fire in their depths—a willfulness and simmering anger that stirred more than lust within him.

Amusement at her headstrong ways? Nay. It was more than that. This was a woman who would fight for what she wanted no matter the cost—

Thor's hammer.

He realized at once why he'd taken her. Why he wanted her. Gwendolyn possessed the strength and spirit that Hedra had lacked—the strength that might have given her enough courage to claim happiness with both hands instead of dutifully doing what her family wanted.

With a curse, he released Gwendolyn's mouth. The noise in the brush had only been a curious hare anyhow. Angry with himself, he vowed he would forget all about the deeper reason he'd been attracted to Gwendolyn once he had her beneath him. She would become any other woman then and this dark fascination with her would be broken. Powerless.

He tugged her forward a bit more roughly than he'd intended. They needed to make better time if they were to reach the ruins before dark.

"I do not wish to be your—pleasure. I will serve no man's pleasure." Her cheeks burned so hotly he could easily imagine how she might look with another kind of flush on her face. Was it from fury? Or did she imagine his touch upon her and resent a stirring?

He hoped for the latter. But either way, he had time to incite the response he wanted. How long would it be before he would see her skin heating with excitement from his touch instead of the mixed emotions she must feel now?

"Are you not a widow?" He did not address her concern directly. Her comment stirred questions of his own. Why would she refuse pleasure when it was offered? He understood her refusal of him. For now. But why dismiss pleasure altogether?

All at once, she fell to the ground, becoming boneless in his grip so that he lost his hold for an instant.

And just like that she ran, limping and slow as a wounded doe after the hunt.

Where was the woman's sense? She was all fight and fire, reflexes and instinct.

"Woman." He jogged toward her, not needing to run any faster than that. Collaring her, he gripped the back of her dress and reeled her backward. "You do yourself greater harm than good. And if you run again, I will carry you the rest of the way like a sack of grain over my shoulder, a position that will be far more enjoyable for me than for you."

He hid a grin, appreciating the vision of that scenario tremendously.

"You do not scare me, Norseman." Her lie could not have been more obvious, but he understood the need to bolster oneself when frightened. "I will escape you, and you will be left with no gold and no pleasure to show for your trouble."

"I am surprised a widow would be frightened at the idea of shared pleasure." He stressed the *shared* this

time, wondering if that had not been clear when he'd
first introduced his intentions.

"You are a heathen marauder," she accused, as if his
choice of gods also made him witless. "Your idea of
pleasure is raping and thieving when you are not killing
Saxons and burning whole towns. I would never share
your pleasures."

"I have never done battle for the blood sport and I
have never taken a woman against her will, even during
the heat of a raid." No man under his command would
dare brutalize innocents during battle. Those kinds of
distractions left a man's sword useless and his back exposed to his enemy.

"That has not been my experience of your people
and I have no reason to trust your word." She trudged
along beside him, keeping pace while her gaze tracked
the tree line nearby, obviously searching for somewhere
to run.

"What of your experience of me?" he demanded. He
had been judged unfairly before and did not appreciate
her assumptions. "I saved you from certain death when
you were about to fall from the castle walls. I have not
harmed a hair upon your head, even when you bit me,
ran from me and hurled insult after insult upon my fathers. What reason have I given you to fear me?"

He flexed his fingers, tightening his grip to encourage
her gaze.

Finally, she peered up at him with dark, thoughtful
eyes.

"Perhaps I have misjudged you as much as you've
misjudged widows." She made it less an admission and
more of a challenge. "Not every widow is eager for—a
man."

At last, he'd learned something about her beyond

her bold spirit. Though the revelation might delay his inevitable seduction of the woman, it provided him with valuable insight. She wasn't merely frightened of the Danes. She'd been mistreated—or at very least unappreciated by the last man who'd touched her.

"Then let us judge one another only on what we know." He hastened toward their destination before darkness caught them alone in the woods with no shelter. "So far, I know you're a brave woman since you ventured out onto the battlements while invaders stormed the beach. I know you think your overlord is an arrogant pig and that you are surprisingly comfortable on the sea."

"You have a fine ship," she admitted. "And I know you disagreed with your men on the way here. They do not approve of your taking me. Also, you are an enemy of the other troops that landed on our shores today. Other than that, I cannot claim much knowledge of you other than that you have uncommon strength and stamina."

He wanted to remind her that those qualities would be beneficial in their pursuit of pleasure, but held his tongue since she hadn't yet grasped how rewarding this would be for them both.

"You see?" Thumping his chest with his fist, he gave her his victory sign. "I am not a man of undue violence."

"But you are convinced you are right all the time and do not accept others' counsel. I suspect your friend from your ship would agree."

She had to mean Erik. And wasn't she an observant one?

"Leading men requires decisiveness." He peered out into a clearing between patches of trees, and when he deemed it safe, nudged her across the open meadow.

"Leading a woman involves *discussion*." She seemed to consider the matter seriously. "And I do not wish to be some object of lust for an overbearing warrior unaccustomed to being denied his smallest desire."

If only she knew what he'd been denied. His home. His rightful place in a noble house. But long before either of those—love.

"This matters naught, Gwendolyn. Because whether you will it or nay, you please me."

TIME PASSED SLOWLY TUCKED against the Norseman's side.

Gwendolyn could not be sure how far they'd traveled, since the journey had a dreamlike quality that made it feel unreal. She had never been so physically close to any man for that length of time. Not once had Gerald slept in her bed a full night. Not once had they taken a long journey together. And while she'd always been thankful that her husband had not spent much time in her presence, traveling with Wulf felt strangely intimate.

At one point, she'd become distracted feeling the beat of his heart close to her own. At other times, shivers shot through her when he lifted her against him to carry her over a treacherous patch of earth. Yes, he'd been oddly solicitous for a man who had the power to harm her. She'd spent most of the trek wondering if he truly believed in this idea of shared pleasure.

A foolish notion. She resented him for planting the concept in her brain when she needed to be thinking about escape.

Considering that she'd been so aware of every moment of the journey to a dilapidated structure near old church ruins, it surprised Gwen that she couldn't guess how long it had taken them to arrive. Now, she sat before a fire in a dusty hearth where Wulf had made short work of starting a blaze.

That had been his first order of business upon arrival. While Gwendolyn searched the small hut for a weapon or escape routes to use once he fell asleep, Wulf then ensured no rats had made a home in an old pallet and settled her among the rushes. The scent of sweet straw and dry wildflowers wafted about her when she moved and she guessed someone must have used the weather-beaten lodging the previous fall.

She'd never spent a night outside a powerful keep before, so she was briefly charmed to think that her pallet had been employed by others. Then, recalling Wulf's reasons for bringing her here, she went back to plotting her escape. Was it foolish to leave in the dark when she had spied no houses on the way?

For now, she decided yes. She had already traveled so far today and it seemed wise to eat before she made another trip. And Wulf barely left the ruins. Even when he caught two slippery silver fish, she noticed he kept his eye on the lodging for all but the moments it took him to plunge his arms into the nearby stream.

Her heartbeat sped up, the same reaction she had every time he neared. Fear? Yes, and yet, she could not fool herself that this was fear she would be raped and left for dead. He could have done that long ago on the beach or forest floor. And he had saved her life from the first.

If he'd not appeared on the wall when he had—as if Fate had intervened—she would not be alive right now full of anxiousness and emotions too confusing to name.

Lesser men might indulge petty violence. Wulf Geirs-son was a leader of men, and a wealthy one at that. He could have commanded far more beautiful women to his bed. For that matter, he could have persuaded many women to do his bidding simply because he was strong and handsome, his compelling azure eyes enticing a woman to comply with his every whim…

"Gwendolyn?"

Her cheeks heated and she thanked the saints for the soft, orange glow of the fire that would hide her discomfort. Had he spoken before now and she missed it? She'd been wrapped up in that disarming gaze so at odds with everything else about him.

"Hmm?" Why was she thinking about other women he'd been with? Why would she care?

"Does your knee still hurt from your fall earlier?" He'd set down near the hearth. Now, he threaded the fish on a thin stick that he mounted between rusting iron brackets that must have long ago held a cauldron.

"No." She tucked her skirts closer to her sides, all-too aware of his nearness. His attention was on her legs even though her skirts covered them completely. "Why?"

What would a brutish Viking care of she bruised her knee? The assortment of scars on his arms suggested he'd taken far worse abuse in his lifetime.

"We might have to move quickly if anyone follows us, and I would not have an injury slowing us down."

She'd forgotten about Alchere. And Wulf's Danish enemy, Harold. Then, there was the threat of her in-laws who still sought control of her fortune through her. To face the in-laws at least, she thought she might prefer to have a merciless, hulking Norseman at her side.

Wulf's voice interrupted her thoughts.

"You will drink." He had dipped a small wineskin into the stream; now he handed it to her.

"Perhaps it is confusion between our languages," she

started, wondering where he'd learned his manners. "But we tend to ask people 'will you drink?' as opposed to telling them they must."

She took the wineskin and squeezed water into her mouth, the icy liquid not doing anything to quell the strange heat that flooded her skin at his attention.

"Ah, but you *must* drink." He reached to wipe a stray droplet from her cheek. "It is important to sustain yourself after a long journey."

Perhaps it was the glittering seriousness of his otherworldly eyes or possibly the heated brush of his fingertips along her skin, but she went very still. Oddly, she feared if she allowed herself to move, she might very well lean toward the Dane instead of away from him. But she told herself that was only because the barbarian represented the only thing standing between her and the wilderness—the only protection she had in the world now that she no longer was under her overlord's care.

Still, her skin hummed pleasantly where he'd touched her cheek and she could not understand why.

The scent of burning pine and savory fish filled the shelter even though a hole in the roof above the hearth allowed much of the smoke to escape. Gwen nestled deeper into the one corner of the room that still provided protection from the elements.

"Even when you know what is best, sometimes it is more polite to offer people a choice in the matter." Her words felt soft and scratchy in her throat, as if she'd not used her voice in a long time.

"I am not the only one who thinks they know best." He settled near the pallet, his strong thighs splayed close enough for her to touch.

You please me.

His pronouncement echoed in her mind, confusing

her when she longed to take refuge in her anger at him for stealing her away.

"You will never have what you seek from me," she warned him. Or did she warn herself? She had no earthly reason to feel this strange warmth when he came near.

"I seek to check your knee." His hands reached toward her and it took a moment for her mind to catch up to his words. "And this I will do."

No sooner had he finished the warning when she felt his hand between her legs.

She arched back, away from his touch, but she'd already scooted into the corner, her spine pressed to the plank wall. Her hands went to his chest, seeking to hold him off or push him back, but all of her strength did not equal a small fraction of his. He merely shifted his shoulders, keeping her arms at bay while his hands made free with her under her gown.

Panic welled as his fingers skimmed up her calves and dipped into the hollow at the backs of her knees where her skin lay bare to his touch. His thumbs stroked a hot path along the inside of her legs.

She expected impatience. Perhaps even violence. But she did not anticipate the gentle probe of his fingers against her swollen flesh. Tenderly, he felt around her knee, front and back. And even though his upper body pinned hers with easy strength, he seemed to use care with his callused hands.

She wanted to protest, but she seemed frozen. Words dried on her tongue as the warmth of his shoulder penetrated her gown about her waist. For a moment, she almost thought he touched her because he wanted to, because he'd decided she should be captive to his pleasure after all.

The notion did not disturb her nearly as much as it should have with his thumb rolling up a tendon toward her thigh. Sweet sensation shimmered along her skin. His scent surrounded her, his potent proximity stirring something deep within.

Her breathing quickened as they stared at one another in silence. The hearth fire popped and hissed. Then, without warning, his bold hands drifted up her thighs, awakening her good sense.

"Nay!" Squeezing her thighs together, she finally found her voice in the odd battle of wills.

If he was going to force himself on her, she would at least make sure he did not touch her without a fight.

He leaned back, no longer pinning her, but not releasing her, either.

"You will bleed from the scratches of my nails," she threatened, rearing back so hard she banged her head on the wall behind her. "You will discover the wrath of the Christian God."

"It is slightly swollen." His voice remained utterly calm, as if he had not heard a single word she'd spoken. "If we need to leave during the night, you will let me carry you so we can make haste."

His hands disappeared from her legs as he rose to his feet, her gown falling back into place to fan about her knees where she sat.

Stalking toward the hearth, he tended the fish, adjusting their height over the flames. She sat in her corner, heart beating wildly, her skin burning from a stranger's impudent touch.

"How dare you." She spat out the accusation with careful deliberation. "You have no right to touch me."

The big brute tugged one fish off the line and downed

half of it in one bite. Then he gathered up the rest of their dinner and brought it toward her.

"You are mine. I will touch you when I like." He unwound a leather strap from his shoulder and pulled free a second wineskin. The scent of mead made her mouth water along with the smoked food. "But for now, it pleases me to wait until you desire my touch."

"You have no honor." Mortification crawled up her cheeks. His hands had roamed all about her knees as if they were wed.

He shook his head and his sculpted mouth frowned.

"I have honored your wish. You said you did not want pleasure and I did not provide it for you," he reminded her, his voice calm and low, a deep undertone beneath her shrill nervousness. "But I think you need it."

Her thoughts reeled. Mutely, she shook her head, unsure how to address this arrogant suggestion.

"Have some mead." He offered her the wineskin, and when she did not immediately reach for it, he took her hand and placed it about the vessel. "Perhaps you need to learn to indulge yourself in small ways first."

She scarcely heard the last bit, her mouth watering at the scent of sweet clover and honey, spiced ginger and the warm, yeasty fragrance of the fermented brew. Lifting the skin to her lips, she drank not just because her belly grumbled for more sustenance than water, but because the complex bouquet of scents reminded her of sweeter times. Before her parents perished, before Alchere had taken control of her father's vast holdings, Gwendolyn had known a life of learning and study. The family keep held a library full of important works and men of education traveled from far-off lands to read the tomes and speak with her father about art and architecture, math and music, philosophy and nature.

Gwen did not often think of those times, the sting of missing the people she loved best in the world too sharp to dwell upon the past. But something in the fragrant mead called to mind the exotic scents that clung to the robes of the foreign men and the spiced dishes her mother would order for their visits. Her parents would have understood the differences between a Dane and a Saxon. They did not know the same boundaries in life that had kept Gwendolyn locked close to Wessex.

"Thank you." She locked gazes with Wulf, passing back the wineskin while her lips still sang with the subtle blend of flavors.

"You enjoy this." He nodded at the wineskin without taking it from her, his gem-colored eyes watching her as if he knew all her secrets. "Take more."

Already, she could feel the effect of the potent brew in her bloodstream. Perhaps it had been a mistake to sip so greedily when she had not eaten all day, but she found it difficult to regret the delicious languor that spread through her limbs. Between the haze of smoke lulling her senses and the steady regard of a commanding Dane, she dutifully lifted the skin to her lips once more and drank.

Sweetness rolled over her tongue. Fire tripped pleasantly through her veins, warming her inside and out. When she lowered the container to the pallet at her side, she wanted to ask Wulf where he had obtained such a delectable brew. But something about the expression on his face stopped the question.

He peered at her peculiarly. Then again, the mead might have dulled her senses enough where she simply could not read the look upon his face. The wine at her husband's keep had been of such poor quality she avoided it still, memories of the stale taste ruining her appreciation for the brew even now. But this—ah, she'd forgotten how delicious mead could be.

Her tongue darted to her lips to wet them, her mouth gone dry after the loss of the libation.

Wulf's gaze tracked the movement, his close attention rousing a sleeping heat inside her that had nothing to do with the mead. Prickly and warm, the sensation stirred awareness of the man before her, a womanly interest she'd never felt for her husband. No matter that Wulf Geirsson was a raider with highly questionable motives, there was a commanding strength about him that any woman would notice.

Any woman would respond to.

As those sea-blue eyes of his loomed nearer, she thought she should pull away to break that enigmatic spell. But her traitorous body did not heed the warning.

When his mouth descended on hers, all thought of retreat vanished.

4

SHE KISSED LIKE AN INNOCENT.

Wulf had not spent much time on the more subtle aspects of lovemaking this past year, his needs fierce but quickly sated by women of both Dane and Saxon blood. Even so, there had been enough kissing to recall that experienced women quickly joined the sensual mating of tongues, their movements sleek and knowing, designed to remind a man what lush rewards could be obtained by a deeper union. But Gwendolyn's advances bore an awkward sweetness, her stillness in his arms suggesting unawakened sensuality more than frozen protest.

He would think about that later. Right now, he absorbed every sweet sigh from her lips as she tilted her chin to allow him better access. Hungrily, he accepted the invitation without ever touching her, unwilling to startle her away now that she offered him such a delectable gift. She'd been so panicked before, when he assessed her injury, that he counted her soft acceptance now as a major victory. A sign he'd been right to choose her for this foray into indulgence.

She tasted like honeyed mead and dark, sensual promise. He stroked her tongue with his and then eased back to capture her lower lip between his. He charged and retreated in this way for long moments, until a soft mew of pleasure hummed from her and she opened to him for a full, deep kiss.

Arousal stirred so fast it made him dizzy. The hard, heavy weight of his want pulled him closer, his heart slamming against his chest with primal desire. He'd taken her for this reason—to test the boldness of the woman on the parapets, to see if she'd fulfill the invitation he'd glimpsed in her brazen eyes. He could find out now. Tonight.

There was no doubt about her willingness. The way she allowed him to lead her, tilting her head where he wanted, her tongue following his while her breasts brushed his chest. He could feel the tight points of her nipples through the thin fabric of her gown.

Why hold back? Whatever reservations she'd had, she'd obviously gotten over them. His muscles hurt from the effort to go slow with her. By now, his head was on fire with images of coupling, her breasts bare, her skirts lifted, his braies open as he sank into her fully.

With the heat of that vision firing him on, he reached for her, his hands molding to the indent of her waist. And even though he'd carried her in his arms before, this was the first time he'd allowed himself to dwell on how she felt. He'd purposely not thought about the womanly shape of her hips before, unwilling to torment himself like that before he could do anything to ease the desire. Now, he pressed her to him and felt the soft give of high, full breasts beneath his chest.

He reached for the shoulder of her gown, searching for a way into the garb so he could feel her skin. But she twisted aside, eluding that touch even though he still held her.

"Release me." She whispered the request so softly he almost didn't hear it until she told him again, louder. "Release me."

He had every intention of following the request. He'd spoken truthfully when he told her he'd not taken a woman against her will. But making his hands follow the command of his brain took time.

"In a moment." He dragged in harsh breaths, trying to ignore the scent of honeyed mead and female desire. "First tell me, why do you deny us both something we want?"

"Now." She wriggled against him with a roll of her hips that would have brought a lesser man to his knees. "Let me go now."

"Woman, you do not help your cause," he gritted between clenched teeth. Still, he managed to relax his grip if only to save himself from the torment of her undulating form.

She scrambled to her feet in the dim lodging. She tried to hurry away from him, but the hem of her skirts caught on the hilt of his sword and she had to wait until he freed her.

With any other woman, he would have enjoyed the moment to tease a caress up her bare calf, but he heard Gwendolyn's rapid breathing and saw her tense stance. He would retreat, for now.

"You must eat," he ordered, pointing her back to the pallet as he moved away from it. "I will feed you fish while you explain why a widowed woman kisses like an untried maid."

The words were a cold splash on her overheated body. Gwendolyn wished to evade the inquiry altogether.

In Richard's keep, none of the other widows—not even Margery—would have presumed to question her first marriage. But if ever the other women took their criticism to an uncomfortable level, she knew if she ignored them long enough, they would cease. And in her husband's home, she'd simply disappeared from his sight, avoiding the hall and locking her bedchamber.

Now, with her thoughts scattered and her skin tingling from Wulf's kiss, she couldn't begin to think of an answer to his query. Here, in this tiny space with just the two of them, there was nowhere to hide and no way to ignore him.

He had her dinner, after all.

Her legs trembled as she walked toward the pallet where she would sleep tonight. There was no fear in her quivering this time. Any man who could pull away from the kiss they'd shared—that was a man with serious self-control. As much as she wanted to hate Wulf for taking charge of her life like it was his right, she no longer feared him.

"If you did not enjoy my kisses, it is just as well." She dropped to the pallet in a billow of skirts and rushes, then tucked the hem of her dress about her legs to keep it secure. "I am no camp follower to entertain you in that way."

She peered up at him expectantly, ready to eat. Her belly growled.

"I did not say I didn't enjoy it." He retrieved the fish from the bed of fresh grasses where he had laid it. Now, flaking off a bit from the center, he steered the morsel toward her lips. "I will never forget the feel of your mouth."

Gwendolyn had no intention of discussing it. She simply nipped the fish from his fingers, careful not to graze his flesh.

"Mmm." The rich flavor surprised her. "It is very good despite the lack of spices."

Safer to speak of the meal than the interlude that had preceded it. He stared at her for a moment as if deciding whether to press the matter, then seemed content to let her change the subject.

"Spoken like a Saxon," he scoffed, scooping up another bite. "All of your spices usually hide the taste of bad fish. If your men were not too lazy to hunt every day, your cook would not need to salt away the flavor."

Gwen took another bite and another, liking the way the slightly crisp outside hid a tender interior. Her senses were all heightened, her body still simmering with awareness.

"Who would have guessed a fierce warrior chieftain would prepare better fish than a keep's cook?" She sipped the water he'd brought in earlier, wondering if it was only her hunger that made the meal taste so good.

"A warrior provides for himself every day he is not seated in his hall." Wulf held another piece of fish at the ready for her, but this time, he did not offer it. He reached forward with his other hand and gently brushed something from her lower lip.

Warmth glowed inside her like a hearth fire turning to embers.

"Then I will not fear starvation under your care." She tore her gaze from his and focused on the morsel that awaited her. "Although you do not dole out the portions as generously as I might like."

She had only meant to tease him into feeding her. She had not anticipated the sudden stillness that came over him or the slow, deliberate stroke of his finger down her cheek to caress her jaw.

"I will provide all that you wish when you are ready."

His voice steamed along her senses, the deep tone vibrating through her skin and making her most secret places hum.

Slowly, she understood his meaning. He referred to the carnal intentions he had toward her. With incredible masculine arrogance, he seemed to think she would one day welcome his touch even though they were enemies. Even though he held her against her will. Even though she had never enjoyed coupling.

As much as she did not wish to discuss the topic they danced around, perhaps she needed to make her position clear so there were no misunderstandings.

"I will never be ready for—" she struggled for words "—what you want from me. I realize the kiss might have been misleading, but it only happened because…" She did not want to have this discussion, but in light of their situation and because Wulf did not strike her as an entirely unreasonable man, she told him the truth. "I had never kissed a man."

The revelation did not appear to surprise him.

"Your husband did not consummate your marriage?" He fed her more fish as he asked the question and she appreciated the small distraction from the embarrassing discussion.

"He consummated it." The morsel soured in her mouth. Her wedding night had been a nightmare she would never forget and she'd been very aware of the moment in which her virginity had been torn from her. "But he never kissed me as you did. In fact, he never gave me anything resembling a kiss, so I was caught off guard earlier by…what we did."

She had been overwhelmed by Wulf, actually. The sweetness of it had been such a surprise, she'd felt immobilized, unable to pull away from an experience that should have been hers as a married woman. Indeed, she'd wondered if Margery's husbands had used their mouths so sweetly and if that accounted for the widow's haste to return to the altar. Of course, Gwen could not see how even the sweetest of kisses would make up for the pain of the marriage act.

"Your husband was unkind." Wulf stated it as if he knew it as truth, though Gwen had told him no such thing.

"I was to be a peace-weaver between warring clans, but I and my husband never saw eye-to-eye despite my efforts." And they had been numerous. "Instead of weaving peace, I served as a reminder of how much my husband despised my overlord."

As she took the last bite of fish to tide her over for the night, she hoped that now Wulf would understand her reluctance to engage in the bedroom games other widows apparently found enjoyable.

She watched as he washed his hands and scrubbed a damp linen over his face now that her meal was finished and his had been consumed long ago. If she had not known the brutish acts men were capable of, she might have been swayed by Wulf's harsh masculine appeal. The firelight played over his bare upper arms, glinting off the silver arm torque and exaggerating the dark shadows in the hollows beneath his muscles.

And, as he stood to make room for his bedroll in the small space, she remembered how large he was. He'd sprawled beside her pallet for much of the evening, his size masked by the lounging.

Besides that, he did not use his size to frighten her. She understood this well after being wed to a man who did just that. Wulf would have dwarfed her husband, and yet he did not lord his strength over her.

"Gwendolyn." He knelt on his bedroll now, his tunic loosened but not off. "You did not mention your mother. Did she not tell you how it should be between a man and a woman?"

There it was again—that warm glow deep in the pit of her belly, a sensation different from anything she'd felt before save with her captor. Neither fear nor pleasure, the tingling awareness felt more like anticipation or perhaps wariness.

"My parents died on the road to Rome the summer I turned thirteen." She had not been such a restless soul before their deaths, but afterward, she found herself wondering about the lives they'd led and adventures they'd had. "They were well-read and well traveled. They invited scholars to our home to read my father's books and study with him. My mother was more inclined to speak to me about the culture of the Greeks than my future marriage. Of course, I was still a girl when she left."

As Gwendolyn laid her head upon a pile of fresh straw, it occurred to her that her mother would have never spent a moment of her time stitching rose petals on bridal garb. The thought made her smile as she remembered how she'd been all but imprisoned with the other widows this morn. Despite her fears and discomforts today, at least she was not stuck indoors, ducking verbal barbs from women who did not like or understand her.

"If your mother had lived until your wedding day, she would have told you that coupling should never be painful." Wulf's voice traveled the short distance between them, bridging a few hands' span so that it sounded like he rested right beside her. His words were so intimate and so unseemly that she closed her eyes tight to shut out the awkwardness of hearing such a thing from the barbarian leader who'd stolen her.

"If she had told me that, I would have only learned the truth soon afterward." And wouldn't that have been all the more wretched? To think mating would bring pleasure only to find out it was fraught with pain?

Weariness overtook her as the firelight died and fresh night air blew through the shelter. She breathed deep, liking the clean smells that were so different from the ancient, musty dampness of her overlord's keep.

"One day, you will know otherwise," Wulf continued, though he seemed content not to argue for now. "One day, you will discover that the pleasure of a kiss is only the beginning."

The smoky promise in his voice called to mind the way she'd felt when he brushed a hand along her cheek or thumbed a crumb from her sensitive lower lip. The kiss he'd given her had awakened feelings she'd not thought possible. But where could it lead? Only to more hurt.

She had to think coupling with a man of Wulf's size would harm far more than it had with her husband.

"Gwendolyn." He had a habit of speaking her name as if he enjoyed the sound of it. "When the day comes where you are ready for more, you will see that the pleasure of a kiss is but a small thing compared to the knee-buckling bliss of what I can give you."

Before he'd made that outrageous claim, she had been tired and ready for sleep. But with the puzzle of knee-buckling bliss to unwind, she found sleep didn't come for many hours and even then, her rest was disrupted by visions of herself weak with wanting in Wulf's arms, her whole body soft with desire for pleasures she'd never known.

WULF AWOKE TO A CRACKING TWIG somewhere in the distance.

He'd slept outdoors often enough to rest peacefully through routine animal sounds. Something human approached or he would not be wide-awake. Had Alchere sent men after Gwendolyn?

Wulf picked up his blade and strapped it to his belt on the hip opposite his axe. He did not carry a sword except on raids, an axe being far more useful. With a last glance through the dark at Gwendolyn where she slept in a pale patch of moonlight, he slid through the cabin door in silence. Outside, the moon rode low on the horizon, spilling misty illumination over the scattered trees and rocky outcroppings that dotted the landscape. Places to hide were few and Saxon men did not understand stealth. Why did he see nothing out of the ordinary?

"Wulf." His name rode the breeze, emanating from a copse of trees to the east. "I bring you supplies."

Wulf grinned in recognition, even knowing those supplies would come at a price. From the group of trees, Erik stepped into the light, holding a satchel in one hand.

He walked freely toward his friend, appreciating that only another Norsemen could have moved so quietly through the undergrowth.

"Come." Wulf waved him forward, grateful there would be no battle to awaken Gwendolyn. "Thank you, friend. What news?"

He stalked through the trees to meet him, taking the bag from him. While he was grateful for the small food stores and other items, he knew Erik would not have risked seeking him out if he did not have good reason.

"We were not in the settlement an hour before Harold sought us out." After handing over the goods, Erik dropped to a stump to sit and opened his wineskin for a drink. "He searches for you."

"He seeks me constantly." Wulf had departed his homeland to avoid Harold, who had demanded vengeance for his sister's death. And Wulf had indeed been responsible. A fragile creature, Hedra had been Wulf's brother's wife, and he knew his refusal to marry her after his brother died had driven her to take her own life.

For that reason alone, he had not met Harold's challenge. Harold was a good ruler and if they were to face each other, Wulf would win and Harold's people would suffer. But it seemed a year of Wulf's absence had not soothed Harold's fury.

"This is different." Erik clamped a heavy hand on his shoulder, a gesture of equals he would not have made in front of the others, but which was his right as his cousin. "He is changed, Wulf. He neglects his kingdom to search for you, chasing the trail when he hears of your raids. Now that he has found the settlement, he will hound us until we lead him to you."

Erik's hand slid away and Wulf understood the seriousness of this new dynamic. It meant a confrontation was close. It also meant Harold's kingdom would look to Wulf as their leader if he unseated the previous ruler.

"You are sure you were not followed?"

Erik thumped his chest in proclamation of his strength.

"I move as the wind moves."

"Nevertheless, I heard your arrival." Wulf peered around the clearing more carefully.

"No warrior is your equal. Harold sleeps in a soft bed after too much mead." Erik rested a hand on the hilt of his sword.

While Wulf's tribe always stood out as warriors among other men, they were as committed to intermarriage and peace as their brethren in the settlement and back home. They came to establish trade routes and increase wealth all around. They fought only when they found resistance.

"You should return before the dawn." Wulf guessed the run had been a long one since the settlement was not close. "The best way for us to reunite might be at sea and I regret that I do not have a vessel. If you do not hear from me in three days' time, take to the water on a morn when the mist rolls thick and I will steal aboard in the cover of fog."

Nodding, Erik turned to leave and then looked back.

"The men believe your Saxon captive is your new concubine."

"So?" Wulf was not surprised, considering the circumstances in which he'd taken her. And while he did not know what would happen with Gwendolyn, he planned to deliver on his promise to teach her pleasure.

"If it is true, they believe she was an expensive one since they were not able to take women, as well." Erik's words did not accuse, but they did convey a tense mood among the men. "And if it is not true, you might consider protecting her with your mantle since she has stirred resentment already."

Without another word, Erik disappeared into the night. Wulf did not call him back as there was little to dispute. He should not be surprised that his followers would be disgruntled to expend their time and expertise obtaining a woman for him. But they did not understand that he'd been drawn to Gwendolyn more powerfully than he'd been drawn to anything in his life.

He did not understand the meaning of it, either, but he knew better than to ignore the Norns when they wove your fate around you. Gwendolyn of Wessex had gazed down upon him from the battlements for a reason, and he would not part with her until he discovered why.

5

GWENDOLYN CAME AWAKE SLOWLY.

She remembered sleeping fitfully through the night, a spring chill waking her frequently so that she'd been forced to burrow deep into the straw pallet and yank the wool blanket she'd been given more tightly about her. She'd been aware of Wulf beside her, but not close enough to touch. That had been fortunate, certainly, although occasionally she'd gazed upon him as he slept and thought about how much warmth his large, muscular frame must emit.

And wouldn't she be so much more snug if she could slide a bit closer to that natural source of heat?

Right now, however, as the first purple hint of dawn slid into the high windows of the cottage, Gwen realized she *was* warm. At some point during the night she had apparently solved her problem of a persistent chill because at this moment, she felt cozy and toasty, her body cocooned at just the right temperature.

At first, she assumed Wulf had given her another blanket. But as the dreamy haze of sleep receded, she began to realize the warmth at her back was alive and breathing.

Wulf's expansive chest fit tight to her spine.

The discovery was so startling, she had to stifle a squeal. She put her hand to her lips to keep in the sound while her brain cataloged the rest of this new situation.

If Wulf had not slept, she would have wrenched away immediately. But since they must have lain this way peacefully for some time, she could not resist the chance to inventory every facet of the warm arrangement that had kept her so comfortable despite the chill.

A thick, strong arm wrapped around her, his hand flat upon her belly. Hard, male thighs backed up to hers, her buttocks nestled into Wulf's lap. What shocked her most was the sword-straight ridge of his manhood pressed tight to the curve of her bottom, the tip of which nudged the base of her spine.

She was familiar with male anatomy, obviously. But since her husband had never achieved this condition without exercising it immediately—at least not that she was aware—she found it intriguing that the Dane slept beside her so peacefully.

Realizing his mood could become dangerous upon waking, she planned to extricate herself from his arms soon. But she could not deny the sense of warm contentment she knew here. And surprisingly, she experienced the same stir of feminine interest that she had during his kiss. The urge to arch back against him went against all reason, yet it persisted.

Carefully, she shifted her hips, following her instincts while it remained safe to do so.

"Do. Not." The Dane's voice growled low in her ear.

Yelping in surprise, she scrambled away from the seductive heat to the other side of the pallet. She yanked a blanket with her, clutching the wool to her breasts. She peered back at him over her shoulder, then flipped around to keep an even closer eye on him.

"Good morn to you, Gwendolyn." Her warrior captor remained still and seemingly in perfect control of himself. "I cannot ever recall waking so pleasantly."

A predatory smile fired her blood, but he did no more than watch her. He looked like one of his pagan gods, his dark hair cascading to his shoulders, his massive arms strong enough to take on the world.

"It must not have been all that pleasant since you chased me away." Her cheeks heated to consider he'd been awake while she'd experimented with him, learning the feel of his body.

"I know my own limits as a man." He rose up on one elbow, the pendant of a hammer about his neck sliding along a leather thong as he straightened. "Given what you went through in your marriage, I thought you would appreciate knowing them, too."

She eyed him curiously. She never would have guessed he neared his limit since he lay so still.

"I am grateful." Unable to will herself out of bed, she cradled close the feelings of that morning. Wulf's scent remained on the blanket. The memory of his body pressed to her back burned in her thoughts. She could recall the shape of each muscle and the outline of every inch.

And the memory was not unpleasant in the least.

"I will recover soon. Perhaps you can distract me until then." His crystal-blue eyes seemed to catch all the light in the room, glinting brightly despite the dimness. "You can tell me how you became a widow."

"I'm sure it wouldn't surprise you to know that my first husband—Gerald—died in a raid by your people."

She had not seen the fighting, but his men had told her of the skirmish on the beach and the damage done by the Danes.

"Where?" Wulf appeared distracted now, the story capturing his interest as he sat up the rest of the way.

"Gerald's keep is called Fanleigh on the eastern shores." She had hated her life there, from the cold, incessant rains to the illiterate war-mongers who filled the great hall. "And although he did not treat me well, he gave honor to his name in death by defending one of the village women from being carried off by a party of marauders in search of Saxon slaves."

She took some small comfort from the knowledge that his final deeds may have redeemed a soul dark with other stains.

"In a way, he died defending you, as well." Wulf tossed another blanket over her legs. "By protecting that one woman, he ensured the safety of many others."

"I never thought to look at it that way." Had Gerald's willingness to die for that woman's safety discouraged the invaders from taking other women? The idea helped soothe old resentments she still carried about her marriage. It also demonstrated a kindness on Wulf's part that she had not anticipated. "Thank you."

She tugged the blanket up to her chin, her skin cooling quickly now that she'd pried herself away from his warmth.

"It is never too late for a man to redeem himself." His eyes glimmered with new fierceness.

She wanted to ask why he said it with the passion of the damned, but he rose to his feet and stalked out of the ruins.

Apparently, that discussion had ended. And for the second time in as many days, Wulf Geirsson had treated her with noble restraint, releasing her even though he'd told her more than once he wanted her.

You please me.

If that was the case, he walked away from her so that she could make her own decision about whether she wanted him or not. Whether she wanted to find out if there could be more to the marriage act than the pain she'd known previously.

The kisses she'd shared with him assured her she had missed out on the most magical aspects of lovemaking. But how could she give herself to a perfect stranger, even if she was admittedly curious about the way Wulf made her feel?

She would not be the kind of woman that Gerald had kept on the fringes of his hall—a concubine. And what else could she call herself if she allowed this heated curiosity to capture her imagination?

Rising from her pallet, she folded her blanket and watched Wulf through the door, her gaze following his every move while he took his axe to a dead tree. Each swing vibrated with the power of his strength, his expression ferocious. Did he work off frustration over her? Or was this punishment to the tree related to those cryptic words before he'd left the cottage?

It is never too late for a man to redeem himself.

What kind of redemption did Wulf seek? From the way he swung the blade, Gwendolyn guessed that his time of reckoning must be approaching.

THE HEAT WAS ON.

Wulf stoked the fire outside the ruins that night, hoping the blaze would help ignite warmth in his captive. Thoughts of her had plagued him all day.

From the moment he'd woken with his arm full of

womanly curves, he'd wanted her. Memories of the way she'd arched back into him, instinctively seeking the kind of fulfillment she didn't seem to have ever experienced, rolled through his head like endless waves battering the shores of his restraint.

Why had he chosen this widow of Wessex for his foray into indulgence? Other women would have been more easily seduced. His standing among his people would have made him a natural target for female attention anyway, but even as a younger man, he'd known that women found him pleasing. Yet he'd been drawn to a widow who'd learned to fear sex, someone who did not even possess the innate curiosity of a virgin since Gwendolyn thought she knew exactly what happened in the marriage bed.

He stoked and ruminated, turning logs in the fire pit until a blaze lifted half the height of the crumbling stone hut, the wavering flames dancing in a spring breeze as dusk fell. Behind him, he sensed Gwendolyn's arrival by the soft drift of subtle fragrance—a soap she used, perhaps, or a floral herb she packed in her wardrobe.

"How is your knee?" He did not turn around to face her yet, requiring more time to steel himself for the powerful draw of her.

"Almost ready to dash for help." She faced him across the fire, placing herself where he could hardly ignore her. "How far could it be to the next farm or village? Surely any Saxon will take pity on a woman on the run from a Dane."

"You will not run away." He needed to be clear on this point. "The dangers are too great. We are far from civilization here."

"I tried to escape you before." She folded her arms. "Why do you think I would be scared to try again?"

"Not scared." He put down his stick near the pit and pointed out the seat he'd arranged for her by dragging a log out of the woods. "But you are too wise to flee food and shelter for the hardships of the wilderness. Thieves and beggars pose far more dangers to a lone noblewoman than a Dane who has treated you fairly."

Settling herself on the log, she tucked her skirts about her legs as if to keep away the bugs or perhaps to stay warm. She eyed their dinner with obvious interest, her gaze alighting on the array of fresh fish roasting on a wet hickory plank he'd split.

"In your defense, you haven't let me go hungry."

Clearly, this counted for something in Gwendolyn's accounting.

"It is my intention to take excellent care of you." He would put her worthless husband to shame. No matter what soothing words he'd used to ease her mind about the man's untimely passing, Wulf felt naught but cold anger for any warrior who would use his might to harm a female. Especially a woman whom he'd sworn to protect in front of his god and witnesses.

"That is what I am beginning to fear," she admitted, turning her dark brown gaze toward him in a twilight quickly fading to black. Her eyes glittered at him, sincere and anxious.

"You worry I will treat you so well you won't want to leave?" He liked this idea more than he should. He could not even pull into a port of his homeland without risking bloodshed. What would he do with Gwendolyn if he found he could not part with her at the end of three days' time? Still, he did not know if her heart might soften toward him, but he found he wanted that very much. Thoughts of her giving herself to him willingly were as addictive as good mead.

"I worry that your idea of treating me well involves things I am not ready for." She spoke so quietly—as if she feared his reaction—that it made him furious anew with the man who had taught her such reticence.

"Gwendolyn." He withdrew the blade he'd just sharpened that afternoon and—once he had her attention—he drew it quickly across his palm. A thin, red line appeared. "By my blood, I swear I will never hurt you." He reached for her hand and held it in his, allowing his life force to seep into her skin along with the vow. "On my life, I will protect you."

He had shed blood for far less. But she looked at him as though he'd lost his wits, her eyes wide with mild horror. Then, perhaps as the words he'd spoken settled in, he thought he glimpsed a fleeting moment of understanding. Appreciation?

She nodded jerkily and he wondered at the emotions that ran beneath the surface of the bold face she showed the world.

"I will hold you to your word, Viking." Her thumb smoothed across the place where he bled. "And I thank you for it."

A momentary hoarse note in her voice told him his gesture had not been wasted. They sat together, hand in hand before the warmth of the blaze, a new promise binding them as surely as any touch. The temptation to kiss her ran hot through him, the need to erase all memory of her cursed husband pushing him hard. But since intimacy seemed to make her more nervous than excited, he opted to seduce her another way.

Easing their palms apart, he leaned toward the fire to check the fish.

"Hungry?"

GWENDOLYN'S BALANCE FALTERED like a just born colt, her heart and mind unsettled by the new facets she'd uncovered of her conqueror.

Wulf Geirsson had vowed to protect her with a blood oath that had all but moved her to tears. Not even on her wedding day had Gerald promised her anything with such earnest passion.

Wulf had also shown her he could retreat when aroused, something that Gerald had suggested a man was physically incapable of doing. Clearly, it depended on the strength and will of the man in question. Wulf, she was discovering, seemed a man with a limitless supply of both.

Yet he'd made his desire for her obvious and forthright, something that—as she considered it rationally and not from a place of fear—was actually very flattering. In truth, she had thought about his kisses and touches all day long, her body assailed with vivid, sweet memories at the oddest times.

And it wasn't just her mind that traveled back to sensual moments they'd shared. Her whole *body* recalled the way Wulf made her feel, surprising her with heated flushes and tingling in unmentionable places. Her daydreams had been wildly inappropriate and wickedly delicious at the same time.

"I'm starving." She searched for the eating knife he had given her eagerly, grateful to pry her thoughts away from Wulf and the fluttery feelings he inspired. "I fear my appetite may match yours this eve."

She did not miss the predatory gaze he cast upon her.

"It does not even come close." Raw, masculine interest lit his words. "But I can always hope."

He turned back to serve them, leaving her shaky and

breathless, but not frightened in the least. Something about that promise he'd made gave her a new security in being around him. She would bet the whole of her wealth that Wulf Geirsson had never broken an oath before.

They ate in silence, chasing down bites of succulent fish with the fresh creek water. Later, as she licked the last of the meal from her fingertips, an unexpected thought occurred to her.

"It seems strange to me that just yesterday, I threw my embroidery down and complained heartily over the mundane boredom of such pursuits while the men stood on the walls and prepared for battle."

"Maybe you have a warrior's heart."

"Nay." She shook her head, understanding herself better than that. "I have an adventurer's spirit like my mother and father. They wandered far and wide while I've been tethered tight to my overlord's home or my husband's home my whole life. Yet now, I sit outside under the stars, far from home, experiencing exactly the kind of thing that I longed for then."

"You are having an adventure." Wulf poured himself a cup of mead from his wineskin and raised the vessel. "Here's to new quests and safe voyages."

"You are quick to toast my exploits, but not as fast to share your strong potion tonight, I notice." Her mouth watered at the memory of the taste. "Is that part of your vow to protect me, I wonder?"

She did not know what madness prompted her to ask when his potent libation had kept her spellbound through his kiss the previous night.

"You are in charge of your own adventure." He handed her the cup, the scent of clover and honey intoxicating her before she even took a sip. "And I do not think a bit of mead will do you any harm."

His deep voice wrapped around her in the dark, the sound as pleasing to her ear as the dinner had been to her tongue. She had been surrounded by the high chatter of unhappy women who did not really like her for so long that Wulf's rich tone, punctuated by periods of total quiet, soothed her.

"Thank you." She sipped carefully, respecting the power of the brew after the experience of the night before. Still, the spicy magic infiltrated her veins quickly, infusing her blood with sweet warmth. "I am surprised you have so much left. I thought we drank more last night."

He must have packed his supplies well, in fact, because he possessed more of everything than she would have guessed they could carry. Then again, Wulf had carted her, her bag and his bag the whole way. The Dane was so hearty and strong she almost wondered if he'd wandered out of Valhalla itself.

"The joy of strong mead is that a small amount goes a long way."

"I have learned this well." Grinning, she took one more sip before passing the cup back to him.

His hand brushed hers as he took it, and the charge that ran through her felt like a lightning strike. This was not an effect of the mead, she knew. Although the fact that her fingers remained there a bit longer than necessary could probably be attributed to the drink and the way it made her blood run thick in her veins like the sweet honey it had been made from.

"Tell me about your family." Wulf joined her on the log, bringing a blanket with him and tossing it over her legs as the night turned fully dark. "You are an only child?"

"Yes." She tucked her hand beneath the blanket to limit the possibility of more accidental touches. As curious as she might be about Wulf and her reaction to him, she was not ready to explore such tumultuous feelings with a man who could offer her no future. "My father was born to a maid of Byzantium, though he was the son of a Wessex lord. He lived there for almost ten years while his father established trade for the king, and he grew up with a fine education. When he returned to his father's home, he sought the best monastery schools to study with the monks and won acclaim for his math and healing. But he was most sought after for his translations. He spoke, read and wrote in many languages."

"What of your mother?" Wulf pointed out a shooting star in the clear night sky as he spoke.

Idly, she wondered if the sight was so common to him that it hardly bore remarking. For her part, she'd never seen the like and her eyes lingered on the spot where the bright flare of light had disappeared.

"My mother told me all of those things about my father's past," she explained, drawing on vivid memories of the woman who had been such a strong force in their home. "She was quick to tout her husband's brilliant mind and abilities, as he was frequently lost in his studies for days on end and was more apt to talk about his latest reading than himself. She was the daughter of a wealthy Mercian house and knew the nobles who patronized my father's work."

Gwendolyn could not recall the last time she'd told their stories and promised herself that she would do so more often in the future. Like the shooting stars, her parents' lives had left blazing trails that should be remembered.

"They sound well suited," Wulf remarked, causing Gwendolyn to wonder if he'd ever thought of taking a wife.

For that matter, didn't the Danes keep wives and concubines at the same time? Gerald had certainly believed that to be so, claiming he'd learned the custom from them.

"Are you married?" she blurted, unable to wait another moment to find out. The thought of touching a man who belonged to another was abhorrent to her, no matter how well-accepted the practice might be in their culture.

"Of course not." His denial was immediate and heartfelt, yet it seemed tinged with an emotion she could not read. Regret? "I have not set foot on my native soil for a year. If I had a wife, I am sure she would be most illdisposed toward me by now."

"But it would not bother you to keep a wife and take another woman to bed?" She had never been a woman to mind her tongue, a fact that had been pointed out to her repeatedly by her overlord, her husband, the other widows…well, everyone.

But Wulf had been forthright with her thus far. Why should she concern herself with social convention?

"I would never wed a woman unless I wished to touch no one but her for the rest of my days." He retrieved the mead and finished the contents of the cup. "So there would never be a question of wanting another."

He replaced the cup in the dirt and stared into the flames. She assumed his thoughts were far away until he turned that clear blue gaze toward her. Then she realized his thoughts were very much here. With her. About her.

Her mouth went dry. Her own thoughts vanished.

Swallowing hard, she finally found an answer.

"That is a noble sentiment." She liked his sense of honor and his passionate avowals.

Indeed, she liked many, many things about Wulf Geirsson.

"My thoughts are for one woman at a time, Gwendolyn." He leaned closer to make his point. "And lately, all my thoughts are of you."

Her breath hitched at the idea of him thinking about her. From the mead in her blood and the blanket around her that held his scent, her world narrowed to him.

"I fear I cannot give you what you seek." As much as she had resented her marriage and the need to bind herself to a man, at least marriage came with a certain amount of respect in the eyes of the world. As a Dane's concubine, she had no assurance of a protector, no legal claim to Wulf. He could simply trade her away when he tired of her… "As a noblewoman, I was not raised to be some man's pleasure thing. My overlord will come for me and then I will remarry—"

"And you could end up with someone just like Gerald. What stops you from finding pleasure—adventure, if you will—with a man who has vowed never to do you harm?"

He had struck a nerve. The idea that she might be living the same life as Margery—dutiful and dry, more worried about well-stitched wedding garments than finding joy in the world—stopped Gwendolyn cold.

"You are an enemy to my king and my people—"

"But not an enemy to *you*. You know this." His eyes darkened to a deeper blue as he spoke. His jaw had grown shadowed with the bristle of his unshaven face. He looked even more dangerous than when they'd first met and yet—not. She knew him better now. "And you must know your Saxons will assume you have suffered the touch of a Dane whether you return to them as pure as the day you left or not. Why cling to someone else's notion of how you should conduct yourself when you have been denied passion your whole life?"

Her heartbeat sped along with the rise in his voice, her feelings soaring in time with his speech. In truth, she did not know why she let anyone else's expectation dictate her behavior when she was in the middle of the woods with a compelling stranger whose kisses roused the sweetest fire she had ever known.

What harm could it do to see where another kiss led when she knew he could stop himself anytime? When he had sworn he would never hurt her?

"It is difficult to remember my reasons just now," she admitted, lured to follow her heart and her instincts.

"Where is the woman I spied on the battlements? The woman who refused to hide during an invasion while her companions cowered in a locked hall?" Gently, he brushed a finger beneath her chin and tipped her face toward his.

The call of passion was too great. In him. In her. In the spring night lush with new life and ancient promise.

"Perhaps she merely waited for the right battle cry." Tentatively, her hands sought his chest, his strength and daring that spoke to her own. Her eyelids grew heavy and fell to half-mast, the intoxication she felt owing everything to the powerful effect of the man, not the mead. "In my case, I think that might be a kiss."

6

IN A LIFETIME OF CONQUERING foreign lands, Wulf had never wanted to claim new terrain as badly as he did right now.

Gwendolyn swayed toward him, bringing with her a whole host of enticements a man could scarcely catalog. The scent of her skin beckoned, the heat of her desire intensifying the fragrance of sweet herbs that she must use for bathing. Her flesh felt soft along his fingertip, firm and tender to touch.

She peered up at him with bold, brown eyes that had turned molten, her shoulders swaying with the ragged breaths she dragged into her lungs.

He wanted her underneath him, on top of him and sideways. But he would treat her with care. He'd made a vow and he would keep it if it killed him.

Then she was in his arms and he couldn't have said who moved first. Her thigh pressed against his, the shape of her leg apparent even through the layers of underskirts and gown. Her hands splayed against his chest, her fingers clutching and clinging to his tunic, as if she could drag him near.

But it was her kiss that brought him to his knees. The

innocent artlessness of the day before had vanished. Her mouth met his fully, hungrily. The reticence was gone, and in its place was a new sensuality. She kissed him like she could not get enough of him, her tongue stroking his with the slow deliberation of a woman who had found a new favored hobby.

He groaned at the feel of her, a full-scale assault on his senses as she arched into him. Whatever else she feared about intimacy, Gwendolyn was a convert when it came to kissing.

Shoring up his restraint, he tucked an arm beneath her legs and hauled her into his lap. He knew better than to rush her, but the sooner she grew accustomed to the feel of him, the better.

She pulled back from him suddenly, her hands framing his face as she stared at him in the firelight.

"I think I will like being in charge of my own adventure," she whispered, her words throaty with newfound passion.

The dazed look in her eyes and the moist sheen of her lips told him she was well on the path to readiness, but he vowed not to rush. He intended to hew to the promise of the blood oath in every moment he spent touching her and exploring her body.

"You must tell me when you feel ready for more," he urged.

Already he throbbed with need for her, her thigh nestled against him so that every movement she made proved delicious torment.

"If you can make it as good as the kissing, I am ready." Her arms wound about his neck, her plump breasts swelling against his chest. "I am very fond of the way you kiss."

He guessed as much from the way she squirmed in

his arms, her body making demands she might not be ready to acknowledge. He could not wait to show her what she'd been missing, what he could supply for her in knee-melting abundance. If he was fortunate enough to share her bed tonight, he planned to ensure she never wished to leave it.

At that moment, it occurred to him that while he'd taken her captive for his pleasure, he had committed himself to hers instead. But he had the feeling doing so would provide him with a new kind of fulfillment.

"You are in luck then." His hands skimmed her sides, slowing to untie the laces of her gown. "For I plan to kiss more of you."

He did not wait for her to consider the implication of that. Instead, he dipped to kiss a place beneath her ear while he further loosened the ties of her gown. A vein in her neck jumped against his tongue and he stroked the spot with care until her head tipped back to give him more access.

The gift of her willingness did not escape him. He had no doubt that she'd been hurt before and it humbled him that she would allow him to touch her.

Would she be so trusting if she knew how much danger awaited them? Harold would pursue him relentlessly. Alchere would call upon King Alfred to help retrieve this woman.

"What is it?" She blinked at him, straightening.

Had she read his mind? Nay. He must have stilled somehow.

"Nothing." He would not let dark thoughts spoil something that should be special for Gwendolyn. Something wild and passionate that would sweep her away on the waves of pleasure like a longship. "I only thought of your comfort. We should go in where there is a pallet and you will be warmer."

Her assessing gaze studied him so hard that he feared she could see straight into his soul. But then, she shook her head.

"Nay." She tugged on the blanket he'd given her earlier to keep her legs warm. "We can wrap ourselves in this and remain under the stars."

Her unlikely proposition chased the last thoughts of an uncertain future from his mind, bringing him fully into the moment with her again.

"You have the spirit of a Dane," he accused, unwinding the wool from her legs and then tossing it on the ground near the fire. "Wild at heart."

He returned his mouth to her neck, lavishing long kisses there until she panted for breath. Then he carried her to the blanket and laid her upon it before stretching out beside her beneath the glittering heavens.

"Give me your hand." She gripped the sleeve of his tunic, showing him what she wanted, and he followed her command, unsure what she had in mind.

As her tongue ran across the place where his blade had cut a thin line, he understood her purpose. She soothed the spot again and again, placing tender kisses there between more provocative strokes.

"The sting is long gone," he assured her, wondering if she had any idea how those deliberate movements enflamed him. "The only ache I feel now is for want of you."

She tensed, her shoulders stiffening as she drew in a small breath.

He'd briefly forgotten about her bastard of a husband, but something about his words had obviously brought her painful memories.

"Gwendolyn." He released her, careful that his touches could never be construed as restraint. "It is a turn of phrase, no more. You could not hurt me if you tried. And a Dane never admits to suffering anyhow." He thunked his chest with his fist in a gesture well-known among his men. "Invincible, you see?"

Her smile was like cooling rain after heated battle, a fresh beginning.

"Touch me more, Viking," she demanded, propping her elbow on the blanket so that she could look down upon him as he lay on his back. "I begin to think I understand the kind of suffering you speak of. It began for me when you allowed the night air to chill my skin."

She had wriggled free of the top half of her gown. With the laces loosened, the shoulders had slid off, leaving the heavy fabric to droop down to her waist. Now her arms and breasts were covered only by the under dress, a thin layer of linen that tempted him with intriguing shadows beneath the pale material.

He dragged cooling breath into his lungs like a drowning man, his fingers itching for a comprehensive feel of her.

Then suddenly, his hands were all over her, cradling the sides of her breasts and palming their full, heavy weight. He stroked up the valley between them with two fingers, then bent to kiss that place. A moan tore free from her throat, but he felt it more than he heard it, the sound vibrating beneath his lips.

Gwendolyn wondered if she might be coming apart at the seams.

Not just her garments, which certainly were falling away as if of their own volition. But *her*.

Control slipped. Defenses flattened. Fear did not even exist. All of the dark emotions she'd stockpiled about men and—this—melted in the light of Wulf's sworn vow, his sensual arrogance and his toe-curling kisses.

She hardly recognized herself, but she liked to think this daring side had always existed. She just hadn't appreciated it since the rest of the world wanted to call her troublesome and outspoken.

Now, the desire bubbled up so fast it seeped right through her skin. A fever took hold of her and she wanted Wulf's lips everywhere at once to soothe it.

How could one man please her so much?

Her fingers tangled in his hair as he fastened his mouth to her breast, tracing the outline of her nipple through the fine linen of her under dress. The damp material clung to her even after he lifted his head to observe his handiwork through eyes grown slumberous with arousal.

Blindly, she tore at the neck of the garment, wanting it gone. Needing her skin exposed to his every touch. When her efforts failed, Wulf slid the linen up, bunching handfuls of fabric in his fingers as he dragged it out from under her gown and hauled it over her head.

Flames leaped in his gaze as he watched her. She knew no shyness, only hunger for his approval. His caress.

"I want to supplant bad memories with new ones." Stretched out beside him under the night sky, she shared the wish she'd made when the shooting star had streaked past them earlier.

She did not understand how his wish for pleasure had become hers, but it had happened and she yearned for fulfillment at his hands.

Wulf took her mouth in his again, as if he knew exactly how to incite more of the heat she wanted. While he kissed her, he reached beneath her skirts and slid his hand up her calf.

Over her thigh.

She could not help a tense moment. This was where Gerald had usually begun his attentions—such as they were. A hand thrust between her legs.

She closed her eyes tightly, not realizing Wulf had replaced her gown.

Disappointment warred with relief. And yes, anger at how a cruel hand could reach from the grave to hurt her even now.

"Gwen." Wulf spoke her name between the kisses she craved so much. "You are not ready—"

"Yes." By the saints, she would not be robbed of her adventure. Her night in his arms before she returned to a world of rules and restrictions, duty and dowries. "Yes, I am. I will not be denied this pleasure you have promised."

She heard the mutinous tone in her voice and he must have, too, for she saw a flash of white teeth in the darkness.

"Tell me, fickle widow, what do you want from me?" He nipped her lower lip and rolled it gently between his teeth before letting it go.

And sweet, merciful heaven. The sensation echoed decadently between her thighs.

"Let me," she whispered, taking his hand in hers and placing his fingers upon her bare calf once again. "I will not be nervous when I am in charge."

She hoped. Nay, she insisted.

Gamely, she slipped both their hands beneath her skirt, her fingers pressing his palm tight to her leg as they slid surely upward.

"You are so soft. So smooth," he crooned sweetly to

her, and she marveled that a man capable of fierceness could take care of her so tenderly.

At the middle of her thigh, she halted, her path unclear.

Wulf tapped the back of her thigh with his pinky finger. "If I cupped your hip, I would press you to me until you were fully ready." He tapped his forefinger on the front of her thigh. "But if I journey north in this direction, I would test your readiness for myself and tease you gently until you begged for more."

Her womb contracted hard at both scenarios, heat sweeping through her like a wildfire until she let go of his hand to concentrate on the feelings. Perhaps she did not want to be in control after all.

"You decide," she murmured, her eyelids falling closed as tension began to coil deep inside her. "I am all yours."

Even before she finished her words, his fingers grazed the damp curls between her legs. She gasped at the feel of him there, patient and attentive, gliding closer and closer to—

Oh.

He grazed the slick folds of her sex, eliciting a moan she hardly recognized as her own. When he did it a second time, she fastened her arms about his neck, clinging to him and the fiery feeling he gave her.

"That is wonderful." Other words came to mind, all in that same vein. Marvelous. Amazing. Delicious. They played over and over in her mind as Wulf pressed harder and her legs parted for him.

If she was tormenting him, he never showed it. She sincerely hoped not, but *oooh*. He knew what he was doing. He had not spoken a single bragging word. Wulf understood pleasure and—

It thundered through her like a mad rush. All her muscles clenched. Held. Tightened. Wave after wave of bliss drenched her insides, breaking over her like the high tide and dragging her down into unimaginable depths.

She knew she cried out because her throat was sore afterward. Her breath heaved her chest as if she'd run up and down the battlements ten times. Liquid pleasure filled the veins where her blood once ran.

"Wulf." She said his name like an invocation, replete with the joy he had shown her.

A joy she'd never really believed existed.

She wanted more. Soon. But for now, she just wanted to soak in the moment and the feelings that—

"Go inside." Wulf barked a command at her as if she was one of his men.

Confusion mingled with frustration. Was Wulf a bit like her husband after all—angry when unsatisfied? Then, she collected herself to notice he was on full alert.

His whole body tensed. Coiled. His hands were off her and at his sides, finding his weapons as he came up to his knees.

Fear didn't just whisper through her. It bellowed.

"Wulf?" Her hands fisted in the blanket as she peered around the dark woods beyond the circle of flames. "What is it?"

"A noise. Someone's here."

With that cryptic statement, he leaped to his feet and darted into the trees, swift and silent. He had the keen hearing of a wild creature, for she had only been aware of the rush of her blood and the fire he'd started within her.

Heart pounding, Gwen blinked away her moment

of happiness and hurried to the cabin. Could Wulf be in danger? If Alchere had come for her, he would kill Wulf on sight. She'd also neglected to warn him about her in-laws. And who knew what cruelty Wulf's Norse enemy, Harold, might wreak if he came upon him alone in the forest.

As the darkness of the cold cottage surrounded her in all its stuffy staleness, she was only certain of one thing. Just now, she definitely did not want to be rescued.

7

THE TRACKS HAD DISAPPEARED at the water's edge.

Wulf rushed toward the crumbling shelter, plagued by the knowledge that someone had come so close to them tonight. This time, it had not been Erik.

His cousin would have remained in the distance and sought him after Gwendolyn slept. Whoever had been in the forest tonight did not wish to be discovered.

Should he tell Gwen what he suspected? That Harold might have tracked them to dole out vengeance over Hedra's death?

Gwendolyn peered from the shelter as he neared it.

"Did you see anyone?" Worry threaded through her voice, her dark brows a flat line in the moonlight.

"No." It was true enough. "But the fire may have attracted attention from thieves and outcasts who dwell in these woods. It may have been a curious vagrant."

"But you don't think so."

The certainty in her voice told him she could read him well for a woman he'd known so briefly. Looping his arm about her shoulder, he steered her back toward the shelter, eager to ensure her safety. The shadows all around them reminded him how vulnerable they were in the dark. He could have taken her back to his encampment, but he'd wanted to have her alone. All to himself.

Now, he cursed the foolishness of selfish desire.

"Actually, that is the most logical answer." He had gone through the scenarios over and over again on the way back here. Harold would never know to look for him in the middle of nowhere without his men. "But there is a chance your overlord's men have found us."

"I doubt it would happen so soon." She ducked into the lodging, her long skirts brushing his leg as she passed, reminding him how thoroughly undressed she'd been when he'd departed earlier. "I do not think he could spare many men to search when he and King Alfred are investing so much in protecting the Wessex borders from you."

King Alfred had proven a most effective deterrent to the Danes. Unlike the Sussex and Mercian kingdoms, the people of Wessex had fought mercilessly against the widespread colonization prevalent on the east coast. Wulf admired Alfred's tactics and found him a worthy opponent, preferring to avoid his army where possible.

"I hope you are right, for I am not willing to give you up." He pulled a set of iron tongs from the hearth and went outside to transfer the hot coals indoors.

When he returned, Gwendolyn had laid firewood in the hearth and swept the ashes. In fact, the entire cottage had been straightened and neatened at some point that day. He had not noticed earlier, but she must have tended those things while he chopped wood in an effort to quell the need for her that had ridden him all day. Could she have been as desperate for distraction as he'd been?

"Do you think it is safe to let the fire burn?" She sat

on the pallet, ensconced in blankets and his fur. She toyed with a small leather pouch he had not seen before. It must have been something she'd brought from her keep.

Something she'd concealed?

"There is no sense hiding from one who has already seen us." He hoped it was a hungry outlaw searching for food. Or even Alfred's army. Wulf would find a way around either. But if Harold had discovered him at last, there would be a reckoning.

He'd paid the *wergild,* man-price, for Hedra to her brother, even though Wulf had not taken her life. It had been a peace offering to Harold and his people since they held him responsible. But Wulf had always known the day would come when Harold's honor demanded Wulf's death. And Wulf, tired of endless seafaring and raiding, had hastened that day yesterday by stealing treasures right under his nose.

Meeting Gwendolyn made him regret rushing Harold's justice. Wulf would not die at Harold's hands in a fair fight. But if Harold attacked at night with his followers?

No warrior could overcome such odds.

"You think someone else follows us."

He looked up sharply at her where she sat calmly, tying the straps of the satchel to a ribbon under the hem of her kirtle. The garment appeared to have been made specifically to hide things. Apparently, whatever was in her pouch was valuable to her.

"Why do you say this?" He stoked the fire enough to keep the cottage dry and insects at bay.

She made a neat knot, looping the tie of the pouch through the ribbon sewn above her hem. Then she flipped her skirts back into place, so that you'd never know she hid things there.

He crouched at the foot of the pallet, hands clasped between his thighs. Waiting.

"You do not seem concerned if outlaws discover us and you know Alchere's pursuit is highly unlikely, yet I can see you are anxious about whatever—whoever—is out there." Her fingers splayed over the fur the same way she'd touched him earlier.

Did he dare let his guard down enough to take her tonight? To return to the pleasures they'd only just begun to explore?

Curse the fates. If his window of time with her was shrinking, he would make the most of every second.

"A Dane is never anxious." He reached to touch her ankle just below the hem of her skirt. Her stocking covered her skin, but there was something sweetly forbidden about touching her there. He ringed her ankle with his fingers like a manacle, then tugged her down the length of the pallet. Closer to him. "But if I give the matter additional thought, it is only because I have a woman in my care to consider. I take that guardianship seriously."

Not allowing her time to think, he stalked her. He stretched out over her, liking the way she did not show the least bit of hesitation.

If anything, her eyes narrowed in sensual speculation, as if she tried to calculate what might happen next.

"You must take good care of me," she demanded, her fingers lifting to the ties of his tunic and loosening them. "I agree completely."

The desire for her that had been interrupted earlier came roaring back tenfold with no more than the soft brush of her fingertips against his chest.

No matter what the future held for them, countries

and worlds apart, he planned to have this night with her—together—to remember forever.

GWENDOLYN COULDN'T UNDRESS him fast enough.

The scare they'd had had given her new perspective on her time with Wulf. It might not last long. If she didn't act now, tonight, she might lose the chance to be touched with tenderness and passion. Why should she not enjoy every moment?

Her hands fumbled awkwardly at ties and clasps, her inexperience apparent. But when she freed him of his tunic, her reward was stark masculine beauty that she would have appreciated even without the glow of the low fire in the hearth.

She recalled an illustration her father had shown her once from a Latin text.

This is a Titan, Gwennie. A race of giants.

Wulf looked like that illustration. The memory had faded and would have been lost if not for this moment with Wulf. He could have walked among the Titans with his strong, straight shoulders and his steely chest cut like armor but sheathed in warm skin that came alive beneath her touch.

She was so enamored by all she'd unveiled that she scarcely noticed her own clothes disappearing until a wave of cool air hit her bare legs. He dragged her under dress up her body and over her head, exposing her completely. Even her stockings had given way to his hands, drooping down her ankles and sliding away from her feet.

"You are much better at this than I," she complained, returning to the fastenings of his braies.

"It is a matter of focus," he explained, as if undressing her were a topic for serious consideration. "I force myself not to get distracted by the prize so that I can work quickly."

He reached to help her with the ties, then arched up to remove the pants altogether.

"I'm afraid there is a great deal more to distract me," she admitted. "In fact, I can't take my eyes *off* the prize."

She marveled at the size of him. *Everywhere.* Her mouth went dry as a whisper of the old reservations returned.

Wulf hastened to lie back down beside her and cupped her chin, forcing her gaze to his.

"Do not worry," he ordered, charming her anew with his oddly thoughtful demands. "You will think about the kisses."

His chest pressed to hers and she felt her body mold to his. Would the rest fit so well?

"I wouldn't have to just *think* about them if you were providing some." She arched up off the fur-lined pallet, her mouth already watering for the taste of him.

"We can start here." His breath curled against her cheek, and she turned toward his lips. Anticipating.

Lightly, she rubbed her mouth along his, hoping it whet his appetite the way it stirred her own.

"But I've got another kiss in mind," he whispered. His feral smile sent sweet shivers over her skin.

She hummed with readiness, her head tilting to one side as his lips grazed her neck. That kiss sent a roll of heat to her breasts, the peaks tightening until they ached. She raked her nails lightly over his shoulders, urging him on. He seemed to follow the trail with his mouth, soothing each place in turn while inciting another beyond reason.

She twisted and moaned at every contact of his lips.

He flicked his tongue carelessly over each nipple, as if he had all day to find the spot that pleased her. Then, when she could bear those teasing strokes no more, he drew her into his mouth, suckling and tugging while heat built in yet another place...

Raw need had her squirming beneath him, ready for more. She gripped his shoulders and lifted herself, attempting to make her wishes known by fitting her feverish body to his. She was ready for this. More ready than she ever guessed a woman could be for coupling.

And for this first time, she glimpsed how rewarding the act might be. Her body craved Wulf.

When he eased back, opening a gap between their overheated bodies, she cried out at the loss. She could see his gaze narrow in the dull glow from the low-burning coals, and she shivered in response. Would this be the moment?

She parted her thighs, willing and ready.

But he did not position his hips between hers as she expected. Instead, he cradled her waist in his palms and slid his hands down her sides. Down, down. She reached for him, wanting the feel of him tight against her, but he knelt between her legs and gave her the most surprising kiss of all.

The shock of it made her squeal. His mouth pressed to her sex, his warm breath streaming over places that ached for a firmer touch. When his tongue darted out along the most sensitive bud at her tender center, she couldn't even think of protesting. Waves of keen sensation blinded her to anything but the exquisite feel of him kissing her there.

At first, she stilled, too overwhelmed to respond. Then, bombarded with decadent delights, she could not help but twist against him. What sweet madness was this? But no power could have stopped her arching hips and clenching thighs. She knew the feel of her completion from his touches before, but this was different. Unique. The coiling tension started again, but this time the release hit her like a thunderstorm, drenching her in lush pleasure so intense she arched like a bow.

The pulsing bliss lasted longer this time, and when the last remnants of sweet contractions undulated through her, Wulf lifted his dark head and aligned his body with hers.

Tremors still rocked her and Gwen buried her face in his shoulder. She could remain here forever, wrapped in his arms and discovering new facets of this fulfillment.

But Wulf's body was not replete with the same pleasure. If anything, his staff had grown all the more impressive in the time it had taken him to ready her. He nudged her swollen sex and teased yet another wave of shivery response from her. While she clung to him, he forged his way inside her.

The raw perfection of the union made her body weep with need even as her spirit mourned the way she'd been treated by another man as a new bride. She had deserved this and gotten so much less. So much worse.

"Thank you," she whispered, her mouth pressed to Wulf's ear as she held on to him. "Thank you."

They were the only words that came to mind, her thoughts so overcome by feeling that it was difficult to hold an idea in her head. Gwen gasped as he responded by withdrawing a short way from her body and then returned in a charge of slick heat. He found a rhythm in this way, retreating and returning, drawing out the pleasure for him and her at the same time. Who knew a woman could feel such a wealth of bliss?

She wrapped her legs tight about his hips and held him to her. She knew what would come next, since this part was one of the few marital rites of passage she'd traveled. Still, even this part held surprises since his charge and retreat renewed her breathless want of him. When the tension wound within her yet again, she began to move, her hips meeting his with each stroke. As she arched up beneath him, she felt his body tense and tighten, his shoulders stiffening under her grip.

He shouted with his release, his fist gripping the blanket beneath her head and his muscles flexing all around her. In that moment, she found her own peak, her body clenching his tighter as the sensation seized her over and over.

Long, silent minutes passed and Gwen wondered if Wulf had had experiences like this before. He knew that she'd never felt anything like it, but she had no idea if their night had been as amazing for him, or if this had been another idle pastime for a man well versed in the language of pleasure.

She hoped for some reassurance on that score, her heart as tender as the rest of her sensitized body. But Wulf remained quiet beside her, his hand rubbing soothingly along her back and over her hair.

As much as she wished to simply focus on the discovery of joys she never imagined, she couldn't help but think about how those joys came with inevitable expectations and hopes.

Before she'd met Wulf, she'd been content with her status as a widow, never knowing what she missed. While she did not long for a husband, a future groom could hardly disappoint when she had such a low standard as Gerald to measure him against.

Now, she resented her time spent in the dark,

oblivious to all that lacked in her marriage. And how would a future husband stack up to the level of bliss that Wulf had shown her?

As his breathing settled into the steady rhythm of sleep, Gwendolyn's heart ached with new hurts and she wondered if she would have been better off not knowing what had been missing in her life. As much as she had enjoyed herself this night, a future without such delights sounded bleak indeed.

Wulf came awake instantly.

He did not know what had roused him, but he stood with his blade in hand near the door of the dilapidated cabin. Gwendolyn still lay on the pallet they'd shared the past few hours, her dark hair spilling in every direction over the blanket below her. Even now, he wanted to tuck her close and pillow her head with his arm while she slept. But if he was sweating across the forehead and holding his sword in the middle of the night, he must have heard something to put him on guard.

Someone must be near the church ruins yet again.

Thankfully, Gwendolyn must not have heard any noise.

He vowed to depart this place with her at sunrise. They had not been as isolated here as he'd hoped and he would not risk endangering her. He hated even leaving her side to seek out the source of the sound that had woken him. What if someone dared to approach the lodging with her inside while Wulf was not there to protect her?

The possibility made him even more tense.

Silently, he opened the front door and slipped out into the night. Dawn still lurked an hour or two out of reach. All traces of the fire he'd made earlier had been hidden.

No embers smoldered. No hint of smoke remained. The few coals inside the cottage must have burned out, as well, the night air clean with the scent of new spring greens.

"Wulf."

The voice called to him from a scant stone's throw away. It did not belong to Erik.

"Show yourself." Wulf tightened his grip on the hilt of his blade. but did not raise the weapon. Any advantage he might gain would be negated if the polished steel reflected in the moonlight and gave away his position.

Who would seek him here? Gwendolyn's men? Or had his crew sent someone besides Erik to speak with him?

"Nay, you cursed bastard." The low voice took on a decidedly ugly note. "I will not be tricked into facing a bloodthirsty, murdering wretch."

The accent was clearer now. Whoever spoke was a Dane, and a bitter one at that. Erik must have been seen returning—one of Harold's men had retraced his path. Wulf eased away from the tree where he'd stood and crept silently along the forest floor in the direction of the speaker. Wulf could not be surrounded by any great number of warriors if this man did not wish to confront him.

"Who wants to know my whereabouts?" He took satisfaction from a scurrying noise nearby.

Clearly, the man was serious about not wanting to face him.

"Harold." The words sounded farther away. The sneaking coward retreated to the east. "He demands your blood for Hedra's life."

Anger stirred along with regret.

"I have paid the *wergild* many times over for her."

He sent home half his earnings from raiding, financing Harold's kingdom and then some thanks to his prowess with a sword and his fearsome reputation. "Is his sister's life worth so much that he will sacrifice his own to my blade?"

He shouted the last to the woods as his quarry ran off to the hills. Toward the settlement where his men quartered alongside his enemies.

Harold could not win against him. Harold's kingdom would be without a ruler and, as the sole survivor of the two highest ranking royal houses, Wulf would have no choice but to return home. It was a fate he wanted no part of. As a younger son, he'd been raised to fight and raid, and it was what he did best. Curse Harold's pride for demanding this course of action.

Curse his own pride for besting Harold at the raid on Alchere's keep.

It had been ill-advised to drag Gwendolyn into the middle of an old feud. But he had not realized at the time how quickly she would become important to him.

Turning toward the cabin, he was surprised to see Gwendolyn in his path. Face drained of color, she stared at him with the same fearful expression he'd spied on the countenances of hapless Saxon villagers when his longship pulled onto their shores.

"You took a woman's life?" Her voice was low, but he heard the slight tremor nevertheless.

Guilt warred with indignation.

"I have taken more lives than I care to recount." He realized that his grip still throttled his sword hilt and he forced his hand to relax. "Our people have been at war many times."

"That was no Saxon man." Her voice gained strength.

Steadiness. "I recognize enough of your strange tongue to know he did not speak of a Saxon woman."

Wulf moved closer to her, remembering the night they had shared. Would she ever look upon him with the same warmth in her gaze as she had then?

With any other woman, it might not have mattered. But this was Gwendolyn, the woman the Norns had put in his path when he had not expected it. Her opinion mattered.

"He spoke of my brother's widow," Wulf explained, tension threading tight along his chest to speak of it after so many moons of trying to forget. "There are some who would say I am responsible for her death."

"What do you say?" Her face remained pale as moonlight as the first streaks of dawn painted the sky.

It was a question without accusation. She did not make an assumption the way so many others had. But then, no woman wanted to think she had lain with a man who might hurt a female.

Ruthlessly, he faced the consequences of his choice to forsake Hedra.

"She lies in her grave because of me." He shouldered past her, unwilling to see the hopefulness fade from her dark eyes. "Come. We are no longer safe here."

She made no reply. But dutifully, her footsteps followed along behind his. He had brought Gwendolyn here seeking pleasure, a reprieve from a year lived by the sword. But he'd known all along it could not last. He could not even claim all three days with her that he'd once envisioned.

No matter how much he wanted to relive the soul-stirring fulfillment he'd known alone with her, Wulf knew the time had come to secure his captive someplace more populated to keep her safe.

8

She lies in her grave because of me.

Gwendolyn turned the phrase over in her mind as she trudged up a sandy rise behind Wulf later that day. Besides convincing him her injured knee no longer bothered her, they'd spoken little since their conversation in the woods.

She had been curious that morning when she heard him leave the cottage. His still sense of listening when he awoke had alerted her that he went outside to chase some danger. Gwendolyn had followed him, thinking she might be of some assistance.

When she'd heard him speak to someone, at first she'd been convinced he must be keeping her closer to civilization than she had previously realized. She'd never expected to hear him accused of murder. Never wanted her first taste of passion to be tainted by the knowledge she'd given herself to a Norseman as bloodthirsty as the ones Saxon mothers warned their children about.

Now, her feet damp with forest dew and creek water, she slogged upward as her heart sank lower. She'd felt too much for the Dane, her heart soaring along with the pleasure he'd given her.

How could her judgment be so flawed that she would find freedom in a barbarian's arms? Perhaps she'd merely responded to the notion of an adventure, and Wulf hadn't been as noble a man as she'd briefly believed.

Memories of his blood oath returned, challenging this new view that he posed a threat. Shaking off those thoughts for the moment, she blinked at their surroundings in an attempt to orient herself.

"This is not the way we came through the forest two days ago," she pointed out, unwilling to follow him blindly when he had hurt another woman who depended on him for safety.

Had he sworn an oath to her, as well?

"My men sailed on to a settlement nearby. We must meet them."

He carried a pack on his back that consisted mostly of blankets and his store of mead. He carried her veil, as well, the valuable garment compacted neatly with his things beside her rings and her father's journal. The roll that Wulf carried seemed surprisingly manageable thanks to the width of those broad shoulders. She'd never seen a warrior so fit.

A tide of remembrances from their night together swamped her. His body had taught hers such wickedly delicious things. Today, her muscles ached pleasantly, her body humming with the knowledge of sensual joys even as her brain shouted cautions and upbraidings.

"Why must we meet them?" she asked, knowing men were not talkative creatures, but finding this man in particular to be short on explanation. "Where are you taking me after we find them?"

Assuming they ever found them. Did these seafarers know how to navigate the lands when their stars did not fill the sky? The sun rose high over the woods just beginning to bloom with new spring growth, and it occurred to her she would not even know which direction to take to return home.

Her skirt caught on the branch of a sprawling bush and she yanked it free impatiently. When she did, she nearly ran into him. He had stopped walking and now faced her. His hands reached to brace her shoulders, steadying her.

The contact had the unnerving effect of making her knees sway all the more.

"I must secure you at my encampment while I settle a score with an old enemy." Perhaps he felt the lightning charge between them, for he set her apart from him with all haste, turned on his heel, and continued his relentless pace.

Gwendolyn fell behind all over again in the time it took her brain to catch up with his words. He wanted to dump her on his followers and leave her there alone with them? It stirred a sense of dark betrayal in her breast to know he would cast her aside so easily.

She hurried forward, scarcely daring to believe the arrogance of this man.

"You would set me aside after amusing yourself with me for less than a sennight?"

The noon sun shone fully upon them as they broke through the tree line and spied the sea.

"Would you rather suffer the fate of the last woman in my care?" He swung around to face her, but this time she was prepared.

The sensual pull was gone, burned away by anger and a hurt that she had allowed herself to care about him. She resented that she could already recognize the scent of him when he walked near.

"Do your vows mean so little to you, then?" She

could see him so clearly in her mind's eye, taking a
blade to his own skin.

And by God, he had treated her tenderly when she
had been fearful of coupling. Where was that man now,
in the bright light of day?

He studied her for so long, his gaze scanning every
inch of her face, that she wondered if he'd forgotten her
question. Then he shook his head.

"All the world fears the Danes." He stated it as in-
disputable fact, his place in the world as assured as the
man himself. "Why not you?"

"You told me not to. Now I would know the truth.
Will you forswear yourself with that vow you made to
me?" Her heart beat rapidly, a hint of fear rising as she
wondered at the fate of the woman in her grave. "Should
I fear you, Wulf Geirsson?"

She would rather know the truth outright. She could
always take her chances and run from him. A village
must lurk closer than she'd realized for him to meet his
men nearby. If she slipped away during the night, might
she find a Saxon willing to help?

The stony set of his jaw did not ease her mind. He
glared at her with his otherworldly blue eyes until she
shifted on her feet.

"Nay." The one word was as harsh as any he'd ever
spoken, yet for some reason, she believed it.

The yearning of a wishful heart, perhaps? He'd shown
her more tenderness than she'd thought possible between
man and woman.

Whatever the reason for her hopefulness, she would
hold on to that belief until she understood this dark
incident in his past. He had treated her more fairly than
her own husband, a fact which bartered him kindness
from her now.

As she watched him stare out to sea, searching for his supporters, she thought about ways to uncover the truth. Lifting her chin into the wind, Gwendolyn sought the coastline for some sign of the Danes, unwilling to relinquish her adventure just yet.

WULF KEPT HIS GAZE TRAINED on the sea to stave off the cursed weakness he sensed in himself where Gwendolyn was concerned. He had treated her fairly and kept her safe. He'd worshipped her body as decadently as if she were his queen, revealing the answers to sensual mysteries that had eluded her until the previous night.

So he had no reason to regret his treatment of her now. He would install her safely with his followers and not think of the Wessex widow again. To do otherwise would merely distract him when he needed to give his full attention to the inevitable battle with Harold. Wulf's destiny would wait for him no longer, and a Saxon noblewoman could play no role in his future. He'd given his heart away once, and the consequences had been more painful than any blow from an enemy blade. He would not get close enough to a woman to repeat the experience and he feared he already cared too much for this one.

He looked back from the view of the sea, needing to lay his eyes on her again before he gave her up. In profile, her face revealed the hints of her father's foreign heritage. The straight nose and dark eyes reminded him of Arab traders he'd met, while her pale complexion and finely chiseled mouth must be the more delicate contributions from her mother.

Looking upon Gwendolyn, Wulf wondered what it would have been like to care for a woman who was unafraid to face obstacles and danger. Would Gwendolyn have risked all for him, if given time? The question was

pointless and only served to torment him with what
he'd never had. And now, thanks to Harold's relentless
demands, never could.

Then, without warning, Wulf sensed a change in the
air. It was not necessarily a sound or even the scent of
danger. It was more like a cold sensation along his skin,
a change in pressure that preceded dark clouds.

Someone approached with stealth.

"Hide," he told Gwendolyn, dropping his bags at her
feet while he reached for his blade. "Do not come out
unless I call for you."

"Do you hear something?" She hesitated, following
his gaze toward the northwest trees where they'd just
been.

"Hurry," he shouted, pointing out a place among the
tree roots against a cliff's edge. "There."

Did Harold's men come for him already? Had the spy
already returned to the settlement in time to orchestrate
a war party?

The sound of horses' hooves built into a steady drum-
roll. Trouble descended like a summer storm as riders
appeared on the horizon bearing a standard Wulf did
not recognize.

There were ten. Fifteen. More. They were Saxons,
all of them. Their dark looks and smaller size marked
them as such.

Too late, it occurred to him that if they cut him
down now, Gwendolyn would be left unprotected. No
warrior's death was a noble one if he left his woman
defenseless.

"By the saints. They come for me," Gwendolyn called
to him from her place among the tree roots. "The banner
belongs to my dead husband's kin."

He listened without acknowledging her, not wanting

to give away her presence. No one but him could have possibly heard her above the din of the hooves. He thought they might run him down until the Saxons reined in their beasts at the last moment, sending their mounts' eyes rolling back as their mouths foamed and dripped.

Wulf did not move, though one of the horses' pawing hooves tipped his raised blade, making the steel clang with vibrations that echoed up his arm.

One of the riders nudged his horse forward. "I am Godric of Fanleigh, brother to the departed Gerald of Fanleigh. Where is the Wessex widow, Norseman?"

Wulf assumed this man led the group. He'd been first to arrive on the hilltop and his helm bore the most elaborate decorations of any of the men.

"Leave it to a filthy Saxon to lose track of a woman." Wulf lowered his blade, knowing he would not have a chance to use it against eighteen men.

If not for Gwendolyn, he would have taken as many with him as he could have before they stilled his sword arm for good. But he could not indulge his pride when he had vowed to protect her. He needed to think of her.

"Where is she?" The fat-faced Saxon repeated. Sweat rolled down his head so profusely, he swiped at it with his sleeve. "Alchere had no legal right to the widow once she married my brother. She was Gerald's bride before that greedy bastard Alchere stole her, and now she will be mine."

Wulf knew Gwendolyn had not made a sound from her nook nearby, yet he seemed to hear her protest in his thoughts. No man who treated his horse cruelly would treat a woman well.

She must be worth an even greater fortune than Wulf had first suspected for her dead husband's kin to devote this kind of force to her return. No wonder she had felt controlled all her life.

The idea of this foul-smelling Saxon touching Gwendolyn gave Wulf the urge to run him through despite the overwhelming odds he faced. He would at least take this man to the grave with him.

"Alchere has protected the woman for many moons since your brother died. How can you claim a widow you do not safeguard?"

"A wife has no right to forsake her husband's family upon his death. She belongs with us. And I will stake my claim the same way you took her." The Saxon unsheathed his sword and brandished it. "By force."

Wulf liked his odds of winning against this man who had come with more ambition than skill. But that left seventeen others. While they were mounted, Wulf fought on foot.

He plucked up his axe with his other hand. There was something about the axe that always made Saxons turn a bit green.

"Try it, and you will die painfully." Wulf let the truth of the statement show in his eyes. He knew how to warn opponents of his prowess. He had not spent his life making war to be beaten by a filth-faced second son who dared to take a woman under his protection. "You have not heard of the stealth of the Danes, I see. While your life blood leaks beneath my blade, your men will have their first taste of the axe at the hands of my followers who blanket these hills in silence."

The falsehood played into the strong Saxon fears and painstakingly perpetuated Norse myth. Warfare by scare tactic could be as potent as any waged with steel.

Their gazes locked. The prickly silence of eighteen men waiting for someone else to blink first was the kind of quiet that always preceded battle. Wulf had experienced it innumerable times.

But when a soft, feminine yelp sounded nearby, he realized Gwendolyn had not. By Odin's hairy beard, the foolish woman rose from her hiding place like a child-size warrior with a death wish. Striding toward him with sharp, determined steps, she cast them both headlong out of the pot and into the flames.

"I am here. I will go with you," she told the drooling, sweating boar pig on horseback. "I pray you, there is no need to shed blood on my account."

A vein in Wulf's temple pounded so hard he thought it would burst. Did she not understand blood would be shed either way? And that her arrival had just made matters infinitely worse?

For the first time, Wulf understood what it felt like to be caught flat-footed on the battlefield. And even as he gripped his weapons, prepared to go out of this world in a haze of bloodshed the like of which these Saxons had never seen, he could not help the wryest of grins.

It seemed the fickle widow of Wessex had developed an affection for her captor. Right now, he could think of no regret he'd leave the world with so great as not getting to take full advantage of that knowledge for just one more night.

9

GWENDOLYN COULD NOT imagine what that hard-headed Dane had to look so smug about.

Fear made her fingers shake like new leaves in a spring gale, her heart pounding so fast she could scarcely catch her breath. Gerald's odious brother, Godric, was a fate even worse than her husband had been. He had been away at wars on the continent when Gerald had died, which had been a blessing since she knew he would have married her within the week. As a second son, Godric had coveted her wealth from the moment Gerald brought her home.

But she could not allow Wulf to face nearly twenty armed and mounted men for the sake of avoiding Godric. To do anything else but give herself to their keeping would be a sure death sentence for the Dane. Seeing him there—ready to protect her to the death—had touched her deeply. She knew instantly she could not live with herself if she did not prevent it.

Now, her gaze lingered on Wulf as she wondered what would happen to him. Would he be free to find his men and live to raid another day? Or would Godric still demand Wulf's life?

She looked from Wulf—cursedly unaffected and gazing upon her with more amusement than remorse for her sacrifice—to Godric, whose eyes traveled her greedily.

She shivered in repulsion, certain the sweating pig would be no more gentle than his cruel brother.

"Release the Dane," she demanded, hoping Godric could not see her fear as she reached the center of the men. "He has not harmed me. I am ready to return to my home in Fanleigh."

The unnerving stillness in the clearing had not been broken. She had the sudden sense that what she'd done had made no difference to the men whatsoever. They waged their battle of wills as intently as before she'd arrived.

Had she put Wulf in an even worse position? How strange to realize that she would regret any harm done to the man who'd captured her by force.

"I will have safe passage for the Dane or I will not attend you." She hated that her voice shook. But by now, she was so scared for Wulf she did not stand a chance of disguising it.

"Gwendolyn." Wulf wielded his axe and his sword as easily as eating knives, yet he spoke her name with the same accented seriousness he'd always used when addressing her. "Thank you."

The words pierced her heart, sounding in her ears like a tender *goodbye*.

Godric urged his horse closer to her. To them. And all his men did likewise. They were surrounded.

"I fear I have made things worse instead of better," she muttered to Wulf, keeping her body between him and the Saxons as the net around them tightened. They would be captured like fish in a net.

"Do not fear," he counseled, his voice as steady as a rock and comforting in spite of everything. "Sometimes we are called to fight no matter the odds when we see injustice that cannot be borne."

This was not the way Wulf Geirsson should die. The memory of him saving her life blazed brightly in her mind. He could have demanded ransom for her or conquered Alchere's keep from within. Instead, he'd merely taken her and a few trinkets, and he'd treated her more kindly than her own husband. How could a man of his skill and resources be lost to a band of green knights who were not worthy to row his longships?

The anger she'd felt at him earlier had faded, replaced by a flood of other memories of him and regret that they wouldn't have more time together.

"Come, Gwendolyn." Godric lunged toward her and she ducked, eluding his grasp. He swore. "You have no right to make demands of me or Fanleigh. My men have traveled long and far to retrieve you."

The menace in his eyes frightened her. He viewed her as his property already.

"Then they are as clod-pated as you," she accused, giving vent to her true thoughts since Godric had ignored her attempt to deal with him civilly. "Richard of Alchere will never recognize a union for me that he did not approve. My family lands never belonged to Gerald, but were under Alchere's care until I bore a son."

Legally, Godric could not take her.

In her other ear, Wulf's voice hummed low.

"You will run when I tell you to."

The words were so ludicrous, she wondered if she'd misheard. Nearly twenty men surrounded them on horseback. Just where did he think she would run?

"Possession is the better part of the law," Godric returned, swooping low to pull her off her feet.

She ducked again, but was not sure she would avoid his arms. Then, a sharp whistling noise passed her ears and her hair ruffled in its wake.

Godric screamed as Wulf nicked his arm with the sword.

"Run!" The command unleashed mayhem like she'd never seen.

Godric wailed atop his horse while the beast pawed the air in fright. The Saxon fell to the ground with a dull thud, holding his bleeding arm. Gwendolyn ran in the gap that opened among Godric's men, retreating to her place among the tree roots. Yet she ran with her head swiveled toward the whirl of dust and swords in the clearing.

Horses and men cried out, the circle of knights expanding and spiraling outward until some turned and fled. She could not quite credit that Wulf would scare off such a large number of men, but she saw him at the center of the circle, wielding the axe and the sword like a man possessed by demons.

His size alone would have made her run had she been one of the young knights who followed Godric. But even if that did not put a fright in them, the way he handled two weapons as adeptly as two men should have. Striking down the group's leader seemed to have thrown the rest of the group in turmoil.

Still, he could only move that fast for so long. Three of the horsemen circled him with renewed vigor, perhaps sensing a better way to attack. Compelled to act, she picked up a nearby rock and hurled it with all her might at the knight closest to her. To her surprise, the rider sank like a stone, puddling on the ground beside his frantic horse. Encouraged, she scrambled for more rocks, flinging handfuls at the knights who advanced on her.

Nearby, some of the fighters who'd fallen back now shouted warnings to retreat before speeding away.

Before she could puzzle out the reason for their hasty withdrawal, a shower of arrows rained down upon their heads. Men fell in their wake, their bodies sliding to the ground in lifeless slumps.

Where on earth had they come from?

Her gaze followed those of the men left standing. On the sea, they found two longships full of Danes. Half rowed the ships. Half strung their bows for another round of arrows.

Wulf's men had arrived.

Relief soothed her for only a moment until she realized their next barrage of arrows could easily down their leader.

"Wulf!" She ran toward him. "Look out! Your men have—"

"They are not my men."

She could not make sense of what was happening. The hiss and whistle of fresh arrows sailing through the sky sent her stomach plummeting to her feet. The deadly downpour pummeled the ground nearby.

Above her head, a shot landed so forcefully that Wulf's arms bent from the blow. Gwen gave silent thanks for chainmail. And then, eerily, there was a scant moment of quiet.

"Come on." Wulf had her hand in his, dragging her back into the cover of the trees where their attackers already hid.

"Godric's men are in there," she warned, her legs

burning with the strain to keep up and the desire to escape the next lethal shower.

Even the sack on Wulf's back had been pierced by the wooden shaft of an arrow. The feathers on the end fluttered as he ran.

"They are long gone," Wulf assured her, his grip so tight on her arm she feared he would drag her behind him if she could not keep up. "We have more to fear from Harold's men."

Her knee screamed in protest where she had recently twisted it, but she kept running.

"Harold?" She knew he meant the Danes. The enemy from his native lands, it seemed.

"Hedra's brother." Wulf peered back and, perhaps seeing her fall behind, paused to scoop her into his arms before continuing. "He seeks vengeance for his sister's death."

The death Wulf felt responsible for. A shiver turned her insides to ice, but she squelched the feeling to focus on survival.

"I can run," she protested, peering over his shoulder, but seeing no one in pursuit.

Later, she would ask him about what happened with his brother's widow. Right now, she just wanted to be somewhere safe—for both of them to live long enough for him to give her those answers.

"Not as fast as I can." He veered sharply back in the direction of the sea, his hands cradling her close against a chest full of rippling muscle, reminding her of his strength.

"What are you doing?" She wanted to hide, not confront these arrow-flinging Danes all over again.

"My men will have tracked Harold's movements. They will know to come for me."

"They weren't exactly helpful back there." Ducking a tree branch, she could not think about those moments when Wulf had been risking his life for her without shivering. "Perhaps they resent your abrupt departure with me."

"They would risk any danger for me." He veered sharply to one side, plunging them into the thickest of undergrowth. "They would have taken cover in a cove or inlet if they saw Harold's men."

She noticed he'd slowed his pace though he paused now and again to be sure they were not followed. Perhaps he thought the enemy Danes would not bother to chase them overland.

"It must be nice to think your friends are so loyal." Her own household was too full of widows vying for every wealthy nobleman in sight. The women were only too happy to cut one another down if it meant stealing more male attention for themselves.

"Treasure-givers attract many followers." He turned sideways down a sharp grade where the sand fell away from his feet with every step.

Tightening her hold on his neck, she realized how natural it had become to rely upon him. Trust him. Did she make a grave mistake to give herself so easily into his care? But then, what choice did she have at the moment?

"Are you suggesting you have bought all that loyalty?" Her skirts caught on a thorny bush and he tugged them free.

The sensation of his hands skimming over her ankles tempted her as much as the strong arm braced under her thighs.

"Not all, but most." His blue eyes bored into hers. "I can be very generous."

Her breath vanished at the thought of his particular generosity toward her. She felt heat flood her cheeks and knew they flamed bright.

He chuckled at her expense, clearly enjoying her embarrassment. She wrenched her gaze away from his to peer out along a cliff's edge overlooking an inlet, unwilling to amuse him further.

"You are a peculiar man to entertain such teasing when a whole tribe of war-hungry Danes seek vengeance on you." His steps lengthened as he moved downward to the water.

Around them, the ground grew slick with moss and muck. The scents of spring turned damp and earthy, peppered with the smell of rotting logs and decaying leaves.

"All the more reason to laugh and make merry if your days are numbered." He pointed downstream as they moved closer to the cove.

There, tucked tight against the shoreline, sat a long-ship filled with men. Wulf's men. The vessel was as fierce-looking as she recalled. The dragon's head at the bow appeared as ready for battle as the crew that filled the dark, low-slung craft. Erik stood at the helm, his wide-legged stance the posture of a man in charge. As they approached, all the men rose as one. They each beat a fist hard to their chests before they sat down again. All except Erik, who glowered at them both.

"The Saxons will come back for her," Wulf's cousin warned, glaring particularly at her.

Clearly, she was not atop his list of favorite people. She swallowed a small lump of fear, knowing Wulf's followers would not feel the same affection that he did for her.

"I will never give her to this Godric of Fanleigh."

Wulf tossed his satchel to Erik. The arrow still pierced the bag and the cousin eyed it warily. "I will leave her at our encampment when I confront Haaraldson."

She recalled his plan to set her aside. To leave her among a foreign people while he settled his own accounts. But then, what had she expected? Of course she couldn't remain with him. He was a warrior and a raider. A leader of men with enemies everywhere. As a Dane and a Saxon, they did not fit together. And yet…she had not been ready to cast aside the tenderness they'd shared so soon.

"You will agree to the battle he's long sought?" Erik wrenched the arrow from the satchel and tossed it in the shallow stream.

"It is time." Wulf waded into the water with her in his arms. "His pursuit has become tiresome and robs me of ever taking a moment's rest."

His crystalline-blue eyes peered down into hers. How long would they have together before he left, she wondered? And what would happen to her once he'd gone? With no protector, would she be at the mercy of his men? Surely not. But she could see no place for herself in the world of the Danes.

There was tenderness in his eyes, or did she just imagine it? Nay. He felt a connection to her that went beyond the pleasurable swell of his muscles melding against her. Today, facing Godric's men, Wulf and Gwendolyn had become more than pleasure-sharers.

They had cared for each other enough to try and save one another. Neither wanted to watch the other die. It was a bond she'd never shared with anyone.

As he set her down in the longship, their moment of connection was broken and she came face-to-face with his cousin. Erik's lips flattened against his teeth in a disproving grimace.

"You have claimed her then? The Saxon is your concubine."

At first, Gwendolyn thought they spoke of someone else. She even looked around curiously for some other female she must have missed seeing. Intellectually, she supposed she must have known this was what she'd become by sleeping with Wulf. But in her heart, she abhorred the practice that had once sent dozens of whorish strangers into her household to make her marriage even more humiliating. At very least, it increased the risk of dreadful diseases.

Yet, she had become the concubine now. No longer a wife with legal rights, but a dispensable plaything for a man's pleasure. The hard stare of every man on the ship confirmed the status she'd never wanted.

Separated from the family wealth that King Alfred held in trust for her son, she was no longer a valued heiress. She'd sunk to the most ignoble of places in Wulf's life, a subservient female who slaked a man's most basic needs.

Would Wulf deny the accusation? Could he protect her now with words as he had done earlier with swords and axe?

As he climbed aboard the ship himself, his dark hair slick with water from a quick swim, he stared hard at the men in his command. His eyes contained the stern warning of a captain and they all understood what he said was law here.

That boded well for protecting her, she knew.

"Aye." With one word, he condemned her to an impossible role. "She is my woman and mine alone."

IF SHE COULD HAVE SLAYED HIM with her dark gaze, she would have.

Wulf had known it from the moment his claim had fallen from his lips. He knew it still applied now as they pulled into his men's encampment many leagues west of Gwendolyn's keep. The trip had been swift. The waves easy and the oars strong.

Now, as night fell and torches were lit all around the small village of temporary huts and tents to welcome him home, he could not enjoy the day's successes with the fury of his Saxon widow surrounding him like a storm cloud.

It seemed she'd come to terms with being a captive, but did not appreciate being his concubine. A prickly woman, his Gwendolyn of Wessex. Still, what else could she be for him? She was the daughter of an important Saxon noble, wealthy beyond imagining. Perhaps one day he would ransom her back to her overlord. But his thwarted love for Hedra had darkened a part of his heart. He did not plan to wed, and if he did, it would be for political advantage in his homeland, not for wealth he did not need.

He moved to help her off the ship as they docked, but before he could get his hands on her, she cast him a dark glare and then dove overboard headfirst into the shallow water.

"Thor's hammer," he shouted, convinced she would not clear the bottom when she landed.

Leaping over the edge, he found the sea deeper than he'd expected as the water rose up to meet him. Reassured that she would not have hit her head, he looked around the ship where she should have surfaced. Where did she think she could go in the dark in a strange land?

Nearby, his men jumped carelessly overboard to reach their women and wine on shore. He wanted to shout at them all to mind their bloody arses before they landed on Gwendolyn accidentally. But he was too busy fighting off the rising fear that something must have happened to her.

She should have risen to the surface by now or else he should have seen her on shore.

"Gwendolyn!" he bellowed.

She had vanished into thin air.

_10_

Freedom.

Had she ever known it until now? Truly?

Gwendolyn swam for all she was worth, heedless of whatever sea monsters might take to the waters at night. Her arms burned with the effort of calling upon little-used muscles, but by God, it was worth it to be free. She did not know where she headed, but the darkness would provide cover and the victory over Godric's men that day had made her bold. She'd hit a man in the head with a rock to defend herself. That decision to take action—a decision that had paid off—reminded her she still had choices. She would strike out on her own to find help and be free of the Danes.

She'd shed her gown and condemned it to the muck at the water's depths, refusing to be hampered by the heavy fabric. She swam underwater in nothing more than her thin shift for as long as possible, hoping to put enough distance between herself and the longship that Wulf would not see her in the darkness. The spring sea was cold, however, and she feared remaining in the water any longer.

And now, pulling herself from the water by the roots

of a tree, she threw herself onto dry land out of sight from the Danes' camp. In the distance, she could hear their shouts and the merry-making of men returning after a journey. Strange music, rich with deep horns and guttural drums, drifted on the water. Closer to her, night birds whistled and called to one another while the waves rolled in at her feet, making shushing sounds as if to tell the rest of the world to be quiet.

And Gwen was free.

The giddiness of the moment could not be dimmed by her shivering or her fears for the future. True, she had no idea how she would proceed with her gown and shoes missing and naught to wear through the forest but a thin undergarment. But she would think about that later. At this moment, she simply wanted to enjoy the knowledge that she had masterminded an escape right under the heathen's nose. He dared to call her his concubine?

Never. When he had wooed her to his bed with his thought-drugging kisses and enticing touches, he had told her she should think only of her own pleasure. But instead of feeling free at following her impulses, she felt more a captive than ever because of his words. He had claimed her in front of his men, declaring her his personal plaything.

The humiliation of it still stung, but she closed her eyes against the burn of tears and reminded herself about her triumphant swim through the dark sea. Blinking her lids open once more, she gazed at the water and wondered what her parents had seen when they'd peered out over such vast expanses. The promise of new lands to discover and people to meet? The lure of intellectual mysteries to solve?

It had been easier for her mother, who'd found a man

who honored her dreams and ambitions. Gwendolyn knew no such man. But at least, for this moment, she knew the taste of independence.

Nearby, a fish jumped, the sound of the splash reminding her she hadn't eaten in a while. No doubt, there was feasting aplenty among the Danes tonight. She had smelled the fragrant smoke of cook fires and the steam of savory sauces when the longship had neared the camp.

Her belly rumbled again, urging her to arise and make plans for the night's shelter and the morning meal. With autonomy came responsibility.

Another splash sounded in the water, and she took it as a sign to begin preparations. But before she could stand, a hand emerged from the depths to take hold of her ankle.

Her scream must have carried all the way back to the longship. She hoped so, because if Godric had followed her here, she would not be able to fight him off unless Wulf—

Wulf.

He rose from the murky waters, recognizable instantly. Even in the dark. Even soaked to the skin.

He did not release her ankle as he hoisted himself up on his elbow. His arrival was frighteningly silent, his crystal-blue eyes vivid in the moon's glow as if they gathered up the scant light and reflected it back at her.

"You found me." She could not contain her amazement, her declaration as breathless as her surprise. "I swam so far."

She peered back out to sea toward where the longship would have been anchored. The distance was formidable. She'd never heard him approach, taking reassurance that he had not called for a search party.

He hovered over her, not relinquishing her ankle until his body covered hers. He dripped on her though he did not touch her. His elbows bracketed her hips, his shoulders blocking out the moon where she sprawled on the sand like a beached mermaid.

He was furious. The emotion had not been immediately apparent since the man seemed to pride himself on maintaining rigid composure at all times. But there was a stormy set to his brow. A determined twist to his sculpted mouth. His nostrils flared as he glowered down at her.

"I will not be your concubine." She had meant it to be defiant, but it came out defensive—the rationalization of a woman neck-deep in trouble.

Make that hip deep. Wulf's chest aligned with her hips, his powerful body appearing just as capable of crushing her as saving her.

"I will not whore for you, only to be flung aside when you go off to raid other lands and steal away other women." She filled the silence while he steadily unnerved her. Did he not understand her motive for escaping?

"Do. Not. Leave. Me." He enunciated this very clearly, as if she were a mere child who might have trouble understanding the meaning.

"You plan to give me away soon enough anyhow," she argued, grateful he'd at least said *something*. She could battle with words. She could not combat silence.

"I will ensure your safety before I depart." He rose higher along her body, forcing her shoulders down to the earth not with his hands, but with her own determination not to touch him. "I will protect you."

The water from the sea sluiced from his body in rivulets and fell onto her. *Drip. Drip.* His tunic clung

to muscles clearly defined. The ties about his neck had
come undone and the placket lay wide open, exposing
his chest and the planks of taut skin over strong sinew.
She swallowed back the ridiculous urge to arch up and
kiss the water from his jaw. His throat. His bare chest.

"I know you are stronger than me and you can impose
your will by force. But I do not have to make it easy for
you. And I do not have to submit without a fight."

The claim might sound ludicrous to an outsider ob-
serving them at a distance—a defenseless maid making
such a bold statement to the outlandishly large Dane
whose body quite literally imprisoned hers.

But even here, with her hair pressed into the damp
sand and his angry eyes glaring down at her, she felt
her own power. She did not fully understand it herself,
this vague and formless feminine strength, but she knew
she possessed it in no small measure with this man. He
did not wish to hurt her. And—more to the point—he
wanted her in his bed.

Not in the way that Gerald had. Wulf did not want to
possess her in anger. The Dane wanted to feel her come
undone at his touch, and this he could not accomplish
any way but with her compliance.

"You made your point," he acknowledged, the words
sounding far more controlled and reasonable than he
looked. "Now you *will* submit. And by your god and
mine, there will *not* be a fight since you want this as
much as I do."

He lowered his mouth to one side of her face and
dragged his lips slowly along the slope of her cheek-
bone. Heat flashed within her like a starburst, strong and
smoldering at the center and sending streaks of warmth
to points beyond.

It was difficult to argue with an arrogant man when

he was so very correct. She wanted Wulf with a fierceness that surprised her, her hunger for him making her back arch toward him like a flower to the sun.

"I will never be yours to command," she reminded him, knowing she must find the will to walk away if he could not agree. "What I give you, I give because I want to and not because you demand it."

His thigh brushed hers, the heavy weight suggestive without pinning her to the earthen floor of spring grass. She nearly came out of her skin. Her thin layer of linen from the sea-washed undergarment was no barrier at all from the stark heat of his body.

"Be warned, I will endeavor to make you want this constantly." He plucked at the shoulder of her damp chemise and pulled the neckline wide-open so that he could see her collarbone and, as he tugged harder, the top of her breast.

It was not easy to maintain the thread of the conversation with his tongue tracing lush patterns down her neck, following the pulsing path of her veins. Thoughts of the future scrambled, her sole concern for what happened here and now.

"Touch me." She brought her hand up to his chest and felt the warmth of his skin beneath the layer of cool seawater that clung to him. "I can think of nothing else."

He halted his kisses to study her in the moonlight. Time stood still as they searched each other's eyes for secrets and truths. The music from the Dane's camp played in the distance, the drums as relentless as the warriors themselves. The sound mingled with the soft roll of the waves near their feet. Stars dotted the sky behind Wulf, a map of lights only a seafarer could follow. Gwendolyn's only guide right now was her blue-eyed warrior, a man who searched for his direction from her, it seemed.

And, ah, he'd touched her more deeply than she'd intended. For instead of charging ahead to put his hands on her body as she'd asked, he sought assurance that she truly wanted this connection with him. And for her stark and ruthless Dane to consider her feelings that way stroked her heart most tenderly.

Blinking back the tide of emotions that threatened, Gwendolyn merely reached for his hand and placed it on her hip, answering his unspoken question.

Wulf felt the sweet invitation of her palm on his skin and released a pent-up breath. His fingers flexed against her waist, savoring the way her hips flared gently from there. Even more, he savored the knowledge that this proud Saxon noblewoman wanted him.

"You lost your dress," he noted, the sight of her skin beneath the delicate linen driving him mad for her. "I spotted you in the moonlight because your skin is so pale."

So fine. So soft. He molded and massaged her hip to fit his palm. Then, leaning more of his weight on her, he edged his knee fully between hers and lifted it to rest against her mound.

Her gasp was a far sweeter music than the boisterous voices lifted in song on the far side of the island. Her fingers tracked a path across his lips, as if teasing him to remember how he'd used his mouth to please her in the past. The soaring satisfaction he took from knowing she sought his kiss and his touch was better than any victory in battle.

"You saw me?" One of her fingers dipped into his mouth and he captured it, licking the salty taste of the sea from her. "My body seems to call for you even when I'm unaware."

A growl of possession started in his throat, roaring through him with such intensity he had to clench his teeth to keep from unleashing it. Instead, he moved his hands, moved over her curves to relearn every dip and hollow, to commit every lush swell to memory.

Her eyelids fluttered and fell shut, her finger stilling on his lower lip, then falling away as she gave herself over to him completely. He eyed her hungrily, her body a banquet of temptations. Through the linen of her under dress, her nipples were tight buds as her breasts strained against the fabric. Unwilling to let her go long enough to pull the garment over her head, he yanked at the neckline with a quick jerk, tearing it easily. She arched up even higher, offering herself to him.

Gladly, he feasted on first one taut peak and then the other. He worked her against his teeth and then smoothed those tender places with his tongue, making her squirm restlessly against his thigh.

She was so hot there, between her legs. He wanted her all around him, to feel that slick heat gripping him as she found her release. But he had to taste her first, had to remember the flavor of her before he lost himself inside her.

"Wulf." She ran restless fingers over his chest and shoulders, reaching lower for more of him, but he eluded her grasp.

His own release was already there, poised and ready in the head of his shaft. He couldn't risk letting her touch him yet. Grinding his teeth together, he fought back the fierce need and kissed his way down her belly, circling her hipbone with his tongue while he spanned the place between her hips with his hand.

The womanly scent of her filled his nostrils. She was all he saw. His whole world narrowed to her and what she wanted. Her need became his.

When he licked a path up the center of her slick folds, she raked her fingers through his hair and down to his shoulders, melting on his tongue. Release hit her so fast she simply clung to him. He didn't let her go until she came, again and again, until he couldn't put off his own need any longer.

She reached for the fastening of his braies, but he couldn't allow her fingers too close to him or he would never make it inside her. He'd put off release so long, and he'd wanted her from the moment he'd seen her slim, pale body swimming away from him in the darkness. Possessing her had been a driving force stronger than he could have ever imagined.

He didn't question it, then or now.

"Come," he commanded, shifting her position so that she was centered on the remains of her torn undergarment. "This will keep the sand off you."

Vaguely, she nodded, following where he moved her. Then her hips arched, demanding more.

He freed his shaft but kept his clothes on to keep the sand at bay. Planting his knees between hers, he entered her in one smooth stroke. She was so wet, so warm and ready, she welcomed every inch of him. Blood pounded in his head more insistently than the cursed drums playing out their war tunes on the other side of the island.

Fulfillment hovered near and he fought it for as long as he could. But then she pressed her soft breasts to his chest and held him against her, enveloping him with her sweetness.

When his release charged through him, he could not

hold back his howl. Never had he wanted a woman so much. Never had he risked all to possess one.

Because no matter what they called one another or how they defined the connection between them, Gwendolyn of Wessex belonged to him as no woman ever had.

And no matter how rational his plan for returning her to safety, he now understood he could never let her go.

11

A DREAM HELD HER FAST.

Gwendolyn knew that what she saw was not real, but she could not seem to wake herself from disturbing visions that plagued her deep in the night.

"Don't," she murmured, clutching Wulf by the tunic to plead with him. "Don't do it."

She was desperate to stop him from something. The emotions felt so real she wondered if she was wrong and this wasn't a dream at all. The passion had fled from Wulf's expression. He was all warrior now—cold and unmoved by her pleas.

But what had she asked him for? To release her? To come back to her?

She tried to ignore the heart-wrenching hurt in her chest, but the scene kept playing in her mind. Wulf refused to look at her. Refused to love her...

"Gwendolyn." Wulf's voice called to her, stern and commanding like the man himself.

Dream and reality blended, the veil between them blurring before it lifted.

She seemed to awaken simply because he wanted

her to, a fact which annoyed her considering how hard she'd tried to snap out of the dream on her own.

Now, they lay in Wulf's bedchamber in the temporary encampment. He'd sneaked her back to the small village of tents, wrapping her in his tunic so that she would not be naked for the short journey. They'd made love on his bed among fine, soft blankets, with a torch burning inside a decorative metal lantern hung from the framework of the tent. The setting had been far more decadent than she would have imagined for the man and she'd wondered vaguely who took such care to erect beautiful surroundings for him that he hardly noticed.

"You were dreaming," Wulf informed her, his real self becoming more distinct from the vision of him in her nighttime imaginings. "You seemed frightened."

He held her close, his instincts protective even deep in the night. Her defenses low while wrapped in his arms, she could not help but confide the truth.

"I wanted something from you and you were so unmoved. I pleaded with you." Gwendolyn remembered the ache in her chest that had felt so real. "But your mind was made up."

She realized she'd gripped his arm and held him fast, the tension from the dream carrying over into her touch. Forcing herself to loosen her grasp, she wondered where such depth of feeling had come from. For so long, she'd felt like she'd been the one held too tightly. Now, she'd wound herself around Wulf like a clinging vine.

Wulf, however, caught her wrist and held it. His dark hair followed the line of his shoulder like a shadow.

"That is what happened with Hedra." His grip was tense. "I refused to listen to her when—"

He appeared more shaken now than when he'd confronted eighteen mounted warriors. His pallor faded and he seemed to see beyond her into the past.

"Hedra." The woman whose death he'd felt responsible for. Would he confide the truth of what happened? "She is the woman Harold fights to avenge?"

He nodded. "I closed my heart to her when she pleaded with me once. I have never forgiven myself."

"Tell me what happened." She drew a tightly woven blanket closer to her neck to ward off a sudden chill.

She did not know if he would tell her. He was a proud man. But the haunted look in his eyes suggested he had not made peace with Hedra's death.

He turned away from Gwendolyn to fill a drinking horn from a heavy silver pitcher beside the bed. He sipped from the vessel and handed it to her.

"As children, Hedra, my brother Olaf and I were inseparable. We were of noble families, but early on, before we understood that their marriage had already been arranged, it was clear that Hedra held a special affection for me."

She sipped the mead, drawn in by the emotions apparent in his voice. He may have grown into a dispassionate commander, but he had not always been that way.

"Hedra and I were adventurous souls, while Olaf was every inch the dutiful son," he continued, his gaze directed toward the flickering torch hanging from the tent roof, but not really seeing it. "Hedra and I kissed once—and more—enough to make me think she would never willingly wed Olaf and that one day we would be together. She begged me for patience while she found a way to tell her family. So, imagine my surprise when she wed Olaf with nary a protest." The hard edge that entered his voice was one she recognized. The hurt

Hedra had dealt him was one that remained with him
even now.

"Perhaps she did not have the strength to disappoint
her family. Every daughter desires to be dutiful." Anything less was a sin. And while the Danes did not recognize the same religious laws, she knew it could not
be so different for them.

A part of her ached for the choice Hedra had been
forced to make, even though Gwendolyn couldn't help
a rising tide of jealousy for the woman Wulf had cared
about so deeply. What would it be like to have a man
care for her that way?

"She would not jeopardize her brother's claim to the
throne." Wulf plucked the mead from her hand and took
another sip before handing it back. "Harold's ambition
was more important to her than her happiness, or mine,
or even my brother's. But when my brother died protecting their homeland from a bloodthirsty neighbor, she
asked me to wed her so that our lands and people would
remain united."

"That is common enough." She could not imagine
why they had not married, why this story did not have
a happy ending. "Godric's family hoped that tradition
would follow suit for us after Gerald died."

"I refused her."

The cold words chilled her. And if that had been their
effect on her, imagine how Hedra had felt if she loved
him?

The heart-wrenching ache in her chest she'd felt during her dream would probably only begin to describe
the pain.

"But you loved her." She did not need to hear him say
it to know as much. He would not have felt so betrayed
by her marriage to his brother if he had not loved her.

"Aye." The word sounded torn from him. "But I could not tell if she asked for the union out of remembrance of happier times, or if this was another facet of her family's ambition. I could not wed for the reasons that drove her."

Wulf watched Gwendolyn blink in surprise, perhaps not understanding how hard his heart had grown during the course of his brother's marriage. But he had loved Hedra, and to his mind, she had spit on his affections with the choice of his brother over him. Why couldn't she have led the life they'd dreamed about? Why did she turn her back on everything she'd pretended to honor?

"So you refused love when at last it was your turn to receive it." Gwendolyn's soft accusation was no more than he deserved. She clutched the horn as if she might need to use it as a weapon against him at some point.

Did it speak so ill of him that he could not trust a woman who had forsaken all the vows she'd made in private to him?

"How could I wed a woman who would not claim me in front of her family and the world just a few years before that? If a strong wind washed up a more appealing stranger on her shore, would that have negated the vows she made to me as easily as her brother's wishes voided those another time?" He shook his head, still not seeing how he could have married her after she'd carved his heart out and expected him to choke it down at her wedding feast.

"How did she die?" Gwendolyn's skin had grown pale and he regretted telling her the tale.

But she deserved to know. Not only because of her position in his life, but also because of her strange dream. Whatever she'd seen in her vision had frightened her. Perhaps the truth would not be as alarming.

"After she proposed a union between us and I refused, she—" His throat turned thick, the memory of finding her as keen as ever. He tried again, needing to put the story behind him. "She took a potion of some kind. She rowed a small boat out into the water and took the draught, then perished at sea. We searched for her for days before someone at a nearby village rode up to say her boat had washed ashore there. She still wore the crown bearing my brother's mark. My mark, as well."

There had been a terrible moment where the messenger had not made it clear she was dead. They had thought she'd been found nearby and could ride to her to bring her safely home. Wulf remembered how his heart had lifted, but he did not know if it had simply been a moment of relief from his own guilt or if he'd been hopeful of amending his harsh words to her. He'd never had time to figure it out before the messenger realized his mistake and made clear that Hedra was indeed dead.

"She was adrift without either of you," Gwendolyn remarked, her gaze faraway as if she rewrote the dream in her mind's eye. "Lost at sea without her old friends." Shaking her head, she bit her lip and seemed to emerge from her thoughts. "I'm so sorry. You must have been devastated, not only to lose a dear friend, but to have an argument between you at the end."

He closed his eyes at the magnitude of the truth. He did not often allow himself to feel it, but he did so now. Somehow, Gwendolyn had guessed at his pain after knowing him such a short time when those who had known him his whole life had never suspected he might grieve for her as much as anyone. The Danes were not a people to express their feelings aloud, but while he was not sure how comfortable he felt sharing this with

Gwendolyn, he noted a certain relief in having told the tale.

"In my land, we honor our warriors by sending them out to sea." Wulf would have never considered Hedra "adrift," but then, perhaps he'd never understood her as well as he'd thought. "I took heart that her final act was one of defiance—to give herself a warrior's honor in death."

Gwendolyn stroked a hand over his shoulder, deftly relaxing muscles he had not realized he'd tensed.

"If she was found far from your homeland, why does her brother hold you responsible?" She tucked her cold toes close to his calves, as if to absorb his warmth.

That gesture, so everyday and universal, connected him to the present instead of the past. He appreciated her quiet support—her trust, even. Not once had she suggested by word or glance that he'd been responsible for Hedra's death.

"Why would he not? Our families were very close and our friendship was common knowledge since I moved into my brother's house after his death to help her. Everyone knew we argued that night."

Gwendolyn wrinkled her nose in confusion, the expression endearing.

"She killed herself." Gwendolyn let the bald facts speak for themselves. "You did not push her boat out to sea."

"My *words* pushed her out to sea, Gwen." He knew it. Harold knew it. Anyone who had been close to their families understood what had happened. "Hedra took her life because I could not forgive her for marrying my brother."

"For this, her brother would kill you?" The rising note of surprise in her voice told him she did not understand.

"You are Saxon. Perhaps our ways seem foreign to you. But there are many who believe he should seek vengeance." Wulf had traveled to many other lands, before Hedra died and since. He knew that the way of the Danes was considered strange to some. Barbaric, even. But his people lived by a code, and he could not break it.

Gwendolyn mulled over this as she finished her mead. Her dark hair gleamed glossy in the torchlight with the curls that had sprang up from her swim in the sea.

He had not told her how much it knocked him in the gut to think of her washing up on shore, dead because of words he'd spoken. Not directly, perhaps. But she would not have dived into the sea if he'd not declared her his in front of all his men. He could not bear another woman's blood on his hands.

"Would he win if he challenged you?" Gwendolyn's question was not what he expected. She glanced sidelong at him, considering. "Would you have to let him win since he is a king?"

"He is a good ruler and a just one. I have hurt the kingdom enough to rob them of his full attention these past years. How could I take the life of their leader, as well?" He shook his head, seeing no answer to a problem he'd thought over many times. "But in a fair fight, Harold Haaraldson could never hope to best me."

"Who becomes king if you were to beat Harold in battle? I mean, what if he caught you unaware and you were forced to fight? Does he have a son who would try to avenge him?"

"Nay. And the kingdom would belong to me. Our

family was to have taken it with Hedra and Olaf's child since Harold's wife has no children."

She handed him back the cup and he set it aside, having lost his taste for mead. He did not enjoy seeing his future spread before him this way. Like a bay with no outlet, he could not see a path that promised fine sailing.

"You would make a fine king," she said finally, turning to fluff the pillow behind her head and settle back down to sleep. "But I admire you for refusing to cut down a nobleman."

Was that what he was doing? There were some among his followers who found his unwillingness to engage Harold cowardly. They did not challenge him on it, as Wulf was not only a strong warrior, but the most effective raiding force their people had ever seen. His men were too wealthy to complain, but the unrest at home had gotten to them all.

"Wulf?" Gwendolyn called to him from the bed with soft invitation in her voice. "Remember that first day, you told me you did not want to plunder for riches, but for pleasure?"

She traced the heavy embroidery stitched along the coverlet where it peeped out from under the fur blanket. Her fingers were long and elegant, a noblewoman's hands. He smiled to think of her tossing aside her own embroidery, her spirit too wild to be tamed by domestic pursuits.

"I remember very well." He had not understood at first why he'd been called to claim one woman alone when her keep had been loaded with lucrative prizes that could have been his for the taking. But the fates had woven a different outcome for their meeting.

"I am glad you decided to indulge yourself. I see now

the weight of your responsibility—to your family and Hedra's. To your followers and to Harold's people. And after bearing the burden of so many expectations, you are entitled to some diversion."

The kindness of the sentiment did not dull the more obvious meaning. His blood rushed hot through his veins, burning away old regret and guilt, leaving naught but red-hot awareness behind.

"Are you offering to be my diversion?" He reached for her under the covers, his hand settling unerringly on her hip. She was so soft, her skin creamy and smooth beneath his touch. Her eyes locked on his and he witnessed the flare of sensual interest.

Would she look at him the same way if she knew he wanted her to remain with him? Or would her aversion to his people's practice of keeping multiple women send her running away again and again?

"I wish to distract you from all your cares, Wulf Geirsson. At least for this one night." She sidled closer to him, her fingers dipping low to stroke up the front of his thigh.

He sucked in a breath between clenched teeth, unprepared for the onslaught of her provocative words and touches.

"You're off to a promising start," he managed, his thoughts dissolving to make room for one overriding concern. "That's definitely distracting."

Her nails skimmed a path of tingling flesh, raking his senses into full swing. He grabbed the errant hand and pulled it out of the covers and up to his lips to kiss each finger.

"Not enough," she contradicted him softly, pulling her hand back and laying it on his chest before smoothing her way down, down. "I want to touch you until you can't think of anything or anyone but me and what I'm doing to you."

He blinked at her bold words. But when her tentative fingers circled the head of his cock, he understood she wasn't merely talking. She had big plans for him.

"Gwen—"

"Shh." She hushed him by pressing her mouth to his in a quick kiss. "I know it's possible because you make me feel that way all the time. I just need to figure out how to—"

Her hand closed around his shaft, and he could not hear anything else she said. Lights danced behind his eyes like a sky full of shooting stars. The self-discipline he prided himself on was nowhere to be found.

"Ah." She hummed her satisfaction, exploring every expanding inch of him with sly, darting fingers. "Perhaps I can learn to tell what you like as easily as you seem to read my desires."

Fire blazed over his skin. He watched her in the torchlight, her dark hair alive with flashes of rich reds and burnished orange. He wanted those long, silken strands sliding over his skin while she tested her new-found sensual knowledge.

Holding himself back required a level of strength he'd never honed on any battlefield. She kissed his jaw and feathered light touches up and down his manhood until he thought his eyes would cross from the temptation.

But then she lowered her lips to his throat, his chest, and the twitching muscles of his abdomen. She could not honestly mean...

"Gwen." Her name was a hoarse plea he scarcely recognized.

"Yes, Viking?" She brushed the softest of kisses along the head of his cock and his control shredded.

"Those pleasures will have to wait." He hauled her upward, her breasts teasing the length of his body as he brought her eye level again.

"Why?" Worry and confusion clouded her eyes. "You do not like—"

"I like." He pinned her to the mattress and stretched out over her, needing to be inside her. He'd passed the point of tenderness about two kisses ago. "But that has to wait until I've had you multiple times in a night and I'm exhausted beyond thinking, and even then—"

He urged her legs apart and found her as ready as him. *Thank the gods.* He couldn't remember what he'd been saying. His only thought was to have her now.

Her fingers clenched his shoulders as he entered her. He moved slowly, not wanting to rush her any more than he already had, but the blood roared in his veins with the hunger to take and conquer, to tame and possess. He cupped her breasts together and kissed them in turn, drawing on the tight buds that beckoned for his attention.

She wrapped her legs around his hips and locked her ankles together, anchoring herself to him. He released her breasts to grip her thighs, steadying her as he drove deeper. Hotter. Faster.

Release rushed through him like a rogue wave, tossing him around until he'd poured everything into her. Sweat slicked his back and washed over him like a Christian baptism.

Something had shifted between them tonight. Both in bed and out of it. He'd revealed things to her he'd never confided to anyone else. In turn, she'd shown him a level of physical trust that humbled him after what she'd experienced with her husband.

She'd been right all along. Gwendolyn of Wessex

wasn't the kind of woman he could take as a concubine. He wanted more than that from her, and he wanted the guarantee that came with a public declaration in front of witnesses. In no uncertain terms, he wanted sole rights to this woman forever.

He knew this as she shuddered against him with the aftershocks of her own release. He understood it all the more as he stroked her hair while she slept.

By dawn, he recognized the path to claiming her wouldn't be easy, especially with a dark past hanging over his head and tainting his future. He wanted Gwendolyn. But in order to have her, he would have to vanquish the ghosts of the past.

12

GWENDOLYN CLUTCHED HAPPINESS to her chest like a secret.

She held it tight as she walked through the dirt paths of the Danes' small encampment, guided by Wulf's cousin Elsa, Erik's sister. Gwen probably had no business feeling so glad when Wulf's people were openly suspicious and resentful of her. Elsa had looked at her as though she would rather tear out her own hair than allow Gwendolyn to borrow a gown, as Wulf had requested.

Apparently, Wulf's people viewed her presence here as inappropriate in any capacity other than a slave. Her ties to King Alfred were not appreciated since the Danes had battled long and hard to establish a presence in Alfred's kingdom.

But with the memories of the tenderness Wulf had shown her the night before to comfort her, Gwendolyn could not be discouraged today. The effects of the pleasure were long lasting indeed, for she felt a new wellspring of joy within her whenever she remembered the delights they had shared.

"Thank you again for the garments," Gwendolyn remarked, undeterred by Elsa's dark glare over one shoulder. "They are very fine. I can trade you a ring for them when I recover my things from Wulf."

Elsa stopped her hurried step to confront her head-on. Almost a head taller than Gwen, the Dane was broader of shoulder and appeared strong as a weaver. Her flaxen hair was harnessed by an unforgiving braid straight down her back.

"The rings that were once yours already belong to us." She spoke clearly in Gwendolyn's native tongue, though the words were heavily accented. "And you are as much our possession as the rings. That is the way of the Danes."

Not even Gwendolyn's relentless good mood could brush off those comments. She wished Wulf did not have to call a meeting of his most important advisers this day. He had assured her the matter was of some urgency, even intimating he might devise a plan for dealing with Harold, so Gwen had agreed to put herself in the women's care for a few hours.

"You've taken my things? The way of the Danes is to steal things without asking?" She fumed to think of strangers touching her mother's rings. And she could not even fathom the loss of her father's journal. Had she risked so much to keep them safe, only to lose them now? She should have left them behind at Alchere's keep.

"Woman." Elsa drew her shoulders back as if gathering steam. "It is enough that you wear garments we labored all winter to craft. Do not think to insult our people because of the weakness of your men to protect their possessions."

Did she need to be so difficult? Gwendolyn bristled at the reminder that she was no better than a possession. An object.

A small crowd had gathered about them. Women traveling to the shore's edge with washing paused to listen. Children darting through tent doors slowed to eavesdrop on the conversation. Even the village elders hushed their chatter around a fire pit to watch.

Gwendolyn regretted her decision to antagonize the woman. She could always ask Wulf about the rings privately. And she would plead with anyone she could for the sake of the journal. But arguing with Wulf's cousin in front of his people would not further her cause.

"I'm sorry." Gwendolyn did not bend her knee to the woman, but she did dip her chin to bow her head in public concession of the point. "I only meant to thank you for the clothing."

While the humility before another woman did not come easily, it was at least accepted. Elsa gave a brusque nod and, gripping her hand a bit more forcefully than necessary, led her on their way.

"You are welcome." Elsa walked shoulder to shoulder with her the rest of the way through the short main street of the village. "You are wise to respect our ways. That will make life easier for you here. We share all that we have and work together to increase our stores. If you are to be one of us, you are entitled to all we have."

They paused in front of the last tent on the makeshift street, a small, humble affair that reeked of incense and herbal smoke.

"I'm grateful." Gwendolyn said as much, but privately wondered why Elsa felt the need to put her in her place in front of the whole village earlier.

"Wulf has brought you here at a difficult time for us," Elsa continued, flipping her long braid behind one shoulder as she waved a greeting to another woman. All of the residents of the encampment were tall and blue eyed, their heritage evident in more than their garb. "Harold has declared open war upon him after Wulf's raid on Alchere that robbed Harold of his spoils. The decision to take you now, when Harold's anger has festered…"

Elsa finished with an eloquent shrug that said more than any words. The Danes resented Gwendolyn because she'd been a catalyst in bringing things with Harold to a head. And no wonder these people were concerned about open war. Wulf might be the superior warrior, but Harold's army severely outnumbered his from what Gwendolyn could tell.

"Do you think he will return me?" Gwendolyn knew Wulf did not wish to keep her, a fact which still tore at her for reasons she didn't wish to think about too carefully. "Or trade me to Harold in amends for taking me in the first place?"

Either scenario frightened her to her toes. She'd found a man to admire in Wulf, but what were the chances any other Dane would treat her so well?

"Wulf chooses to keep you for now." Her pale blue eyes skimmed over Gwendolyn's features as if searching for an answer to the puzzle of why he would do such a thing. "That is not uncommon among our men, but it is unusual for Wulf. He does not tend to take captives in raids."

Elsa turned to open the incense-spewing tent, as if she'd said all that she needed on the subject. But Gwendolyn was more confused than ever. Did Wulf not take captives because of Hedra? Did he still love her?

The idea stung more than it should have.

Elsa waved Gwen forward. "Come. Wulf asked me to bring you here."

Gwendolyn recalled the brief exchange between Wulf

and Elsa earlier. Words had been traded in their harsh, guttural language even though both of them spoke hers well enough. Gwen had assumed that Wulf had merely repeated his order to Erik's cousin to take care of finding proper clothing. But apparently there had been other instructions she'd missed. Had he not mentioned them on purpose?

The happiness she'd been clutching close to her heart deflated a bit in the harsh light of day. Perhaps the things Wulf had confided in her last night had been more to warn her away than a chance for her to understand him better.

"Who lives here?" she asked, following Elsa into the tent.

The question hardly needed to have been asked once she stepped into the smoke-filled hut. The sweet scent of burning herbs was so strong she draped a loop of her hair and veil across her nose and mouth to lessen the potency. From the sticks affixed to the roof hung webs fashioned of rough wool twine. Some of them held beads at the intersection of the weaving, others contained bits of what looked like bone and hair tucked into the corners.

Herbs hung to dry overhead, while on the dirt floor sat an old crone humming and chanting over a small flame surrounded by jet-black rocks. The woman's garb was unlike any other female in the village. The sleeves were embroidered with rune staves, some of which were familiar to Gwendolyn, and some that were not. Either way, it was obvious they had reached the hut of the local wise woman.

"Mother, our guest has arrived." Elsa bowed low to the crone, who paid little attention to her.

Instead, the woman's eyes fixed on Gwendolyn and

she felt a hint of fear skitter up her spine like the spider climbing to its oversize web over her head.

"I'm Gwendolyn of Wessex," she explained, wondering if "Mother" was a deferential title or if the woman was family to Erik and Elsa.

The moment of fear passed when sunlight streamed in through the tent as the door behind her opened. She knew who would be there before she turned. Not even the heavy scent of burning herbs could mask her senses enough to hide Wulf's arrival. She felt the man in her veins, her body instantly alert to him whenever he neared.

She turned to see Erik at his side. The two men entered the tent together. Both of them bowed their heads to the crone.

"Wulf." Gwen longed to reach for him, to take his hand and gather comfort from his presence, but he did not spare her a glance.

Did his kindness to her extend only to the bedchamber? A bit more of the day's happiness dwindled.

"Mother, I ask you to cast the bones for Gwendolyn and for me." He asked this in Gwen's language, so at least he did not leave her in ignorance of their purpose here.

Still, she would have her future read? Gwendolyn knew such an activity would be frowned upon by her priest, but once more she reminded herself of her parents' teachings—the respect for other cultures—and she chased away some of the fear inherent in such an act.

The old woman muttered under her breath, then drew a bag from her voluminous robes and chanted foreign words over them. Then, with the flourish of a great hall performer, she cast the contents of the bag onto the dirt floor where another twine spider web had been carefully arranged in the packed earth.

Swallowing down her fears, she wondered silently what Wulf hoped to accomplish through this. Did he really believe the old woman could see their futures? Gwendolyn did not even like the idea that their futures were available for the woman's review since she preferred to think none of it had been decided yet.

"The Saxon brings wealth and lands." The wise woman pointed a gnarled finger over some of the runes she'd tossed to the floor. Most were red in color, although a few were bleached white around the edges from use. "These you must take."

Did the hag tell him to make war on her overlord Alchere? Or did the woman refer to the lands the king held in trust for Gwendolyn's firstborn son? Alchere oversaw the holding where Gwendolyn had grown up. He'd been charged with its safekeeping when he'd been charged with her upbringing. Did Wulf mean to take the lands where she'd been raised?

Her gaze flew to Wulf. He remained expressionless, his eyes fixed on the seer's work. In fact, Erik and Elsa appeared equally serious and raptly interested as the old woman preached advice that would be deadly for Gwendolyn's homeland.

"Wulf, you cannot mean to—"

"Shh." Elsa hushed her at once, her hand encircling Gwen's wrist like a shackle. She gave a fast shake of her head, eyes full of warning.

"In Wessex, you turn Harold aside, but at a grave price," the crone continued, her high voice creaking with age like an uneven step. "Our people will follow you and your seed proves fruitful."

His seed?

Gwendolyn blinked. She peered over at Wulf once again, but his stoic expression had not registered the slightest disquiet or pleasure. Did the woman refer to her? Could she carry Wulf's child?

For a moment, she wondered if Wulf had taken her to secure her wealth and lands after all. What if he'd known that her dowry was attached to her having a son?

"These are good omens." The wise woman straightened and gave them a toothless grin. "You will prosper well, Wulf Geirsson, but do not delay your preparations. My knees warn me our fair weather will not last beyond the sennight."

Wulf nodded, the only hint of deference Gwendolyn had ever spied in him.

"I will tell the men of the fortuitous tidings. Thank you." He took Gwendolyn's arm as if to usher her from the hazy, sweet-smelling tent.

She gathered her breath and dug in her heels. "You cannot mean to implement—"

"Not here," he warned, his low voice rumbling like thunder in the distance. "Come."

She wanted to call the old woman a trickster and a teller of falsehoods, but the crone had returned her attention to chanting a foreign song and collecting the bones. And hadn't Gwendolyn told herself she would wait to speak to Wulf privately? She just hadn't expected a visit to the tribal sage could possibly turn into a war council with her homeland as the target. Had she understood the wisewoman's words correctly when she told Wulf to take her wealth and lands?

Clenching her teeth together with an effort, Gwendolyn maintained her silence as she followed Wulf out of the tent. He did not lead her back to his quarters, but toward the edge of the woods nearby.

"Gather the men," he called over his shoulder to Erik while leading Gwen away from the encampment. "I will address them shortly."

Stunned into silence, Gwen could hardly find her voice. And when she did, she scarcely knew where to begin addressing the problem.

"You cannot seriously determine battle strategy within a soothsayer's hut." Fear for her birthplace and the people who lived there made her heart race at a frantic pace. "Do you truly mean to wrest my lands and wealth from Alchere? From the king himself? Believe me, Alchere does not oversee all that belongs to my firstborn—"

She tripped on a tree root and he righted her. Unconcerned for her throbbing toe, she clutched his tunic to draw his attention, desperate for some reassurance that he did not mean to wage open war on her homeland. For all that she despised Alchere and always had, she did not want to bring that kind of destruction to the people she'd lived with for many moons.

Wulf's stony expression looked like a man ready for battle, but perhaps seeing her distress, he softened his tone. "Gwendolyn, your overlord sold you off to a man who hurt you and he would do it again without blinking. Do you believe your father's lands are in good hands with him?"

Her overlord had kept her all but imprisoned, guarding her like a fire-breathing dragon guarded gold.

"But what of your rule?" She could not believe she even considered it as a possibility. "You would unleash the furor of the Danes on innocents who never asked to serve Alchere? And why would you follow the advice of a wise woman who has never lifted a sword?"

Nearby in the village, Gwen could see people filling the main street through the huts as they made their way toward the shore where most of the warriors already gathered. A hum of excitement filled the air for these vagabond Danes, while Gwendolyn felt naught but despair.

Wulf frowned. "The wise woman speaks for our ancestors in Valhalla. She does not tell me what to do, but relays the guidance of my fathers. It is always up to the leader to decide how to use their wisdom."

"But you have already decided." Gwendolyn's heart cracked at the thought of him taking over her keep and bringing many wives to fill the halls with blue-eyed children.

"I need a base to battle Harold and this will be it." He kissed the top of her head, but it felt like an afterthought while his thoughts raced ahead to raiding and conquering.

But hadn't she known all along that was the way of the Danes? Tears burned the corners of her eyes, but she would not be foolish enough to let him see. She hadn't followed her head in caring about Wulf, but had trusted the misleading pleasure he had shown her.

Indignation and hurt washed through her, drawing her down into misery like a rogue wave.

"That is all that concerns you, isn't it? Battle strategy and besting your opponent. It's why you took me in the first place." Releasing his tunic, she straightened to face him, knowing she could not soften toward him again. "Not because you wanted me. You took me so that your enemy could not."

LATER THAT NIGHT, WULF decided when he arrived in Valhalla his first order of business would be to confront the Norns in *Helheimr,* the world of the dark goddess of spinning and weaving, the deepest realm of the Underworld. Would those ancient sisters be able to explain why he had been confronted with the impossible task of protecting Gwendolyn's physical well-being while safeguarding her womanly heart?

Right now, it seemed he could not do both. She was not some tavern maid that he could keep safe merely by providing her with a tent and a meal every day. She was a Saxon heiress coveted by many. Her king and her overlord collected rents on her properties. Her dead husband's family sought the wealth that would belong to the man who fathered her child. Wars were fought over women that valuable. So if he wanted to keep her out of Alchere's hands and out of Godric's hands, Wulf had to install her somewhere with walls and gates, guards and weapons. Thanks to his feud with Harold, he did not have those things. But Gwendolyn did. It made the most sense to take the properties that would be hers one day anyhow.

Yet, this practical need made him appear calculating and greedy in her eyes, just like all the other men who wanted control of her. He'd hurt her today.

He watched her now from the edges of the night's bonfire. His people toasted the warriors in preparation for their upcoming battle. The women gave themselves to the men in private couplings all around the woods, taking hold of precious life while they could and making the most of it. But his fickle widow was apart from the revelry after having ignored him all day.

She currently attempted to steal a horse. Not just any mount, either, but *his.* He wondered why she did not settle for one of the smaller mares that would have been easier to manage. But nay, the woman who strode the battlements during an invasion and dove off a longship into treacherous waters had to choose his oversize, battle-hardened warhorse for her latest escape attempt.

If he thought she might be in real danger, he would have whistled to the horse or intervened another way. Erik watched her from the shadows, as well, his second-in-command helping him protect her. Wulf would have been more amused at the brazen cheek of the woman if his chest wasn't constricted so tight at the thought of losing her.

She truly would leave him.

He hadn't wanted to believe it after the night they'd spent together. He'd told her things he'd never shared with another living soul, claiming her tender heart for his own after having claimed her beautiful body days ago.

He needed to wed her. Not just for legal rights to her keep and lands necessary for his battle with Harold, because he could obtain those by force on the battlefield. But he wanted her to bear his name and his protection everywhere she went. By invoking his name, she could send enemies fleeing.

He wanted her to have that power and that safeguard so that no man would even dream of touching her. But how would he coerce her consent in front of a priest without alienating her completely? Some Danes might force a marriage on a captive, but Wulf would not do that.

He could think of only one way to convince her, but he was not prepared to offer the tender sentiment she might respond to. Hedra had robbed him of that softness, and he would not lie about a love he could no longer feel.

While he brooded, Gwendolyn somehow managed to get her leg over the beast's back. Her soft cry of surprise was echoed by the warhorse's neighing. From the shadows, Erik looked to him, but Wulf was already on his feet to give chase.

He might not want to wed an unwilling woman, but with a fickle widow trying to outrun him at every turn and putting herself in one kind of danger after another, he might no longer have a choice.

13

OF COURSE HE COULDN'T CATCH her on foot.

She rode a swift horse and she weighed no more than a kitten. But that didn't mean he would concede defeat. Wulf called off his cousin with a gesture, then ran toward the stretch of woods where Gwendolyn had disappeared. He vaulted dead logs and a wood cart, his eyes trained on a swath of pale skirt whipping in the breeze off the water, ready to use his secret weapon.

He whistled.

The high, piercing wail brought his mount to an immediate halt and he hoped against hope Gwendolyn hadn't been thrown in the process. Memories of the wise woman's prediction about his children put his heart in his throat. Could Gwendolyn be carrying his babe even now? A child he might have endangered?

A flurry of mild Saxon curses met his ears before he saw her, the passionate oaths reassuring him she couldn't be terribly hurt.

"Gwendolyn." He called to her through the darkness as he spotted the pale linen of her skirts. "Are you hurt?"

"Do even the beasts of the field obey your every

command, Dane?" She ignored his question to ask her own, her words fired with anger.

As he approached the horse and its disheveled rider, he could see the fury in her expression. Her dark eyes flashed in the moonlight as she turned to him, her lips pursed in a tight frown. Other than that, she appeared unharmed. Her skirts were muddied and covered with brush and leaves from the unwise dash through the forest. Her sable-colored hair tangled about her shoulders, her veil ripped away by a low branch and still drooping from the offending stick a few feet behind her.

The clear spring skies had offered her some moonlight, at least. And the mild temperature helped combat the fact that she had not bothered to wear a cloak.

"Thankfully, the beasts of the fields obey far better than Saxon women." Reaching her side, he took the reins of his horse and patted the animal's flank before brushing some of the leaves and twigs from Gwendolyn's skirts. "You must know the years of training that go into a good warhorse. What I don't understand is why you chose the biggest of the lot? Didn't you know he would be the hardest to manage?"

He held out his hands to her and she hesitated. Did she have another plan in mind for escape? Or was she so mad that his touch was now unwelcome? He was surprised to realize the latter upset him more than the former.

Either way, she conceded and after a moment, slid into his arms. The feel of her curves against him was a momentary brush with bliss. Her softness molded to him, fitting him perfectly. Then, straightening immediately, she held herself apart from him.

"I did not think carefully enough. I chose the animal whose neck looked strong and thick enough for me to duck behind in the dark. He is so big that I thought he would keep me safe."

"And so he did." Wulf gave the animal a scrub behind the ears and turned him around to return to the camp.

Moments later, they walked side by side to the edge of the village and handed off the horse to Erik, who was wise enough to then disappear discreetly. Nearby, men and women lingered in sensual leave-taking that would last until dawn. Some couples had retreated to the tents, but the younger ones—the ones who had not staked a permanent claim to each other—took their goodbyes under the sheltering trees at the wood's edge or down by the water.

"Do not let me keep you from joining your friends," Gwendolyn remarked as she hastened her pace toward his tent. "I will not be warming your bed this night."

"Gwendolyn." He reached out a hand to stop her since she would not have answered him otherwise. His fingers clamped around hers and he tugged her back toward him.

Her pulse jumped under his thumb when he rubbed it over her smooth skin. The scent of the dried flowers that had been packed around her gown tempted him to lean close and inhale deeply.

It would not be difficult to seduce her to his will. He knew that as surely as he knew she would resent him for it on the morrow.

"I have never touched you against your wishes, and I would not do so tonight." He used the opportunity to slip his thumb into the sleeve of her gown, to skim the tender skin of her inner forearm. "But it may be difficult for either of us to sleep, knowing we did not take this last chance to touch each other. My people believe the gods favor those who live with vigor and passion. That is why the women seek out the warriors as much as the warriors seek them on the eve of battle."

For some, it would be the last tenderness they knew.

Wulf followed Gwendolyn's gaze to a half-dressed couple straining together under a birch tree a good stone's throw away. Even at that distance, the pale skin of the woman was easily visible under the glow of a three-quarters moon, her shift up to her waist while her lover's hips kept a steady rhythm against hers. Backed against the trunk, the maid's spine arched while her slender thighs gripped the man's sides, her fingers clenched tight about his shoulders.

Gwen clapped a hand over her mouth, but could not stifle her gasp of surprise.

"They do not wish their coupling was more private?" she whispered, tugging her gaze from the couple.

At her wrist, Wulf could feel the effect the scene had upon her pulse, her blood pumping faster. As did his.

"Since we embrace passion and virility, we do not feel the need to hide it." He lifted his other hand to her cheek and stroked the soft skin along her jaw. "But if you have any wish to feel my hands upon you that way, I am happy to keep it private."

Her breathing accelerated, and he savored the quick rise and fall of her breasts as they strained the seams of another woman's dress. His hands itched to cup her full curves and tease the tips to pebbled stiffness before he took them in his mouth.

"You did not think of our privacy when you dragged me to the soothsayer's tent to discover your seed would be *fruitful*." She clenched her fist at her side. "I am not a mare that you can discuss how well I might breed in front of a tent full of people."

He felt the tendons strain beneath his touch.

"I believe that is a standard blessing she bestows on many supplicants. If she sees health and longevity for a man, she suggests he will have many children."

At the time, he had not given that aspect of the woman's words much thought, focusing instead on the necessary battle ahead and what it would mean to put the past behind him.

"I am a noblewoman. I do not wish to be left alone when you go to battle with a babe and no—" she stepped back, away from him "—no legal rights for either a child or myself. It is bad enough that I have no control over my life. I will not pass on that helplessness to a child."

Desire and loss burned within him. He could almost taste her on his tongue. The thought of going to bed without her, without her kiss on his lips or her sighs of pleasure in his ears was more than he could bear. Besides, he could not suffer the hurt in her voice.

The thought of a woman in pain because of him—he would not stand for it again.

"Then we will wed now. Tonight." He had planned to wait until he took her keep so that he could marry her in front of a Christian priest. "If that is the assurance you seek—"

"You only want to wed me to legitimize your claim to lucrative Saxon lands." Her gaze focused solely on him as if she'd shut out all temptation of the sensual couplings around them. "Why would I be comforted to wed a man who only offers such protection after discovering I am an heiress to a fortune?"

Anger stirred. He tried to do something for her and she twisted his every word. The Saxon woman used speech the way Danes used their swords—wielding a weapon of language to confound him. Why could they not seize what they wanted with both hands while life offered them the chance?

"I can take your lands and keep them by the might of the sword, make no mistake." He reached for her, frustration urging him to show her how quickly she would shed all her clothes for him if he backed her up against a birch tree and settled his mouth on hers. "I have not raided and battled for a decade to rely on some greedy Saxon lord like Alchere to honor a marriage contract."

Behind them, a woman called out her pleasure to the heavens, her throaty fulfillment echoing a man's low voice urging her on and on with a rumble of words.

Wulf knew the sound affected Gwendolyn, for she relaxed in his grip, as if her attention floated somewhere besides their disagreement. As if her body remembered the kind of decadent pleasure that made a woman moan like that.

"We should not discuss this here." She swallowed hard, and he hoped that she could envision herself feeling as fulfilled as the woman who'd just cried out.

"Come with me, Gwen," he urged her between clenched teeth, his need crawling up his back with fierce claws. "Tomorrow, I could bleed out on your shores with a Saxon arrow through my gut, and we will curse our stubbornness this night." He tunneled his fingers through her hair on either side of her head, guiding her mouth to his. "You breathe fast and shallow, like a woman who is aroused. Your tongue darts out to lick your lips like a woman anticipating a kiss. And I would wager all of my gold on two continents that your thighs are pressed tightly together beneath your skirts like a woman who would prefer another sort of pressure there—"

She rose up on her toes and kissed him before he

could finish. Her soft mouth molded to his while she wrapped her arms about his neck and squeezed.

He wanted to get her back in the shelter of his tent, but she hooked her hands in the front of his tunic and yanked it open, distracting him. The cool sea breeze blew over his body, powerless to chill the inferno burning away his usual caution.

"Touch me," she demanded, arching against him so that her breasts tempted him beyond reason. "I want to feel the night air on my skin when you undress me."

It was all the concession he needed from her tonight. If she was naked beneath him, she couldn't steal horses or dive off his ships.

Lifting her off her feet, he backed her deeper into the woods. Her bare skin would not incite any man's lust but his when he hauled up her skirts.

He could not be sure how she'd caught the feverish hunger that affected him, but it burned her up. Her fingers unfastened his belt and tunneled under his tunic, her hands splaying across his chest before descending low along his waist.

Finding a solid hawthorn trunk, he settled her against it and went to work kissing her neck and the exposed skin of her shoulders. The ties of her tunic were undone in a trice. He pulled it up and off, leaving her in the same shift she'd worn to swim the sea. Her breasts strained the fabric, the tight peaks vying for his attention.

He wanted to sink to his knees and kiss her through the shift until she begged him for more, but to do so would leave her too exposed. He palmed one of her breasts and nipped the other with his teeth. She cried out, her hands raking through his hair and down his back in silent demand for more.

Would he ever have enough of her?

Need rocked him, compelling him to lift her skirt just enough to slip a hand up her thigh. An answering moan filled his ears, setting his nerves on edge and making his shaft throb.

"Quickly," she urged, her voice cracking with the same desperation he felt.

His tunic fell away. Her nails scratched his chest lightly. Her thigh slid up the side of his and she tugged away the extra skirts impatiently so their hips met.

He sucked in a breath behind his teeth and held it, trying to find a shred of his scattered control. He was used to being in command, to standing apart and issuing orders. Right now, he couldn't stop himself if he tried.

Hunger blindsided him. His hands took over, tweaking a taut nipple to a stiff peak, cupping her mound at the juncture of her thighs. A roaring in his ears drowned out everything except the sound of her erratic breathing and the hum of approval deep in her throat. He kissed and licked her, testing her readiness with his two fingers inside her.

She gasped at the invasion, then murmured a chant of sweet encouragement, her hips bucking against him to take more. He wanted to bring her back to his tent, but they'd waited too late. Too long.

He kept his body between her and the village, even knowing they were too deep in the forest for anyone to see. Loosening the laces on his trousers, he freed himself enough to position between her legs. Then, lifting her up, he parted her sex and lowered her onto his cock.

Her nails bit into his back as he plunged into her, but her feminine core pulsed and squeezed all around him as she came. The rush of knowing he'd pleasured her was a primal satisfaction that made him want to pound his chest and roar with possessiveness.

She was *his*.

The feeling was as fierce as anything he'd ever experienced. His release shuddered through him violently, his hips pumping on and on as he filled her with his seed. She clung to him, legs locked around him, the aftershocks of her own orgasm still making her tremble. Or maybe she came again. All he knew was that it was the most perfect union he could imagine—here in the woods against the hawthorn tree with the woman he would make his forever.

The churn of emotions after years of shutting them off rocked him to the core as much as any release. After Hedra's betrayal—marrying his brother when she loved him—he'd sworn never to love another. He'd stayed true to that vow when he spurned her attempt to become his wife after Olaf died. But now, here was the fickle widow of Wessex with her hunger for adventure and her passionate heart, tempting him to lose years of hard won control.

His skin cooled fast in the night air, the sweat drying on his back as he lowered Gwendolyn to the ground and adjusted her skirts. Gathering their clothes, he lifted her in his arms, still reeling from emotions he had no wish to feel.

"Come." The old control felt like a rusty thing, his voice unsteady as he used it. "We must rest. The sleep before battle is never long enough."

His words were not unkind. However, Gwendolyn must have heard the retreat in them, for the raw joy that had been there earlier quickly faded. Biting her lip, she merely nodded.

Nothing would bring back the closeness of this night.

If they were to have an effective marriage—a practical marriage that would provide comfort and alliance—it would be better if the heedless, raw passion was clamped down into something more manageable. Fondness, perhaps.

But not love. It was the only challenge this Dane refused to undertake.

WAS THERE NO ONE WHO could challenge this champion of the Danes?

Gwendolyn peered around the crowded courtyard of her father's old keep late the next evening in the aftermath of the battle, wondering how Wulf could send an army fleeing in the course of a few hours.

Of course, King Alfred's men had vacated the lands to fight off a Norse invasion elsewhere in Wessex. And Alchere had few soldiers here, not suspecting a battle here at a lesser stronghold than the one he held farther up the coast. So Wulf had triumphed over a small force. Still—he'd wrested away the coastal fortress with precious little bloodshed, the sight of his axe and his broadsword sending hardened warriors scurrying to the four winds.

Now, as Wulf oversaw the banishment of Alchere's men and messages dispatched to Alfred and neighboring lords, Gwendolyn wondered how she felt about his easy victory. Proud? Yes. She could not deny rooting for Wulf despite her anger with him the day before. It was not his fault he was raised to make war and raid any more than it was his fault that Hedra had stolen his heart long ago and neglected to give it back when she'd died.

It was wrong to feel resentment of the dead, but Gwendolyn could not deny that she knew a perverse jealousy of the feelings Wulf once had for someone else. Her death had turned him into the hardened and practical warrior he was today—a man who did not spare time for tender emotions.

She'd read her father's journal for comfort on her way to the Wessex keep a few hours after the battle, reminding herself how her parents favored understanding other societies' customs and never assuming one tradition or religion was better than another.

And seeing how Wulf's men strove hard to do his bidding, she suspected he would be a strong and fair leader. But she worried what the victory meant for her. For them, if he truly planned to wed her.

"He is clean for a Norseman, I suppose." Lady Margery stood beside Gwen, sniffing the air as if testing the truth of her statement. "No doubt you could have done worse than that one."

Gwendolyn's nemesis had taken up residence at her father's old keep after the raid on Alchere's stronghold. Apparently, all the widows had been transferred here while repairs were made on Alchere's walls.

Gwendolyn kept silent, wishing she'd suggested they banish Margery along with the outgoing soldiers.

The widows had been called out to the courtyard in addition to the Earl of Alchere's steward and one of the king's envoys who'd remained behind until Alfred's proposed return in a fortnight. Wulf would make arrangements for all of them before he allowed his men to take their ease in the great hall and celebrate their victory.

It was impressive to see them assemble there, some still bleeding from the short skirmish that won the day, not moving a muscle until Wulf released them. Of course, Gwendolyn now understood how important that tight rein was for Wulf. She had seen a hint of his control slip last night and she felt his regret afterward like a tangible thing. Would he ever show her that wildness again?

Watching him now, his face expressionless even as he gave his men permission for a victory cheer, she could not imagine it.

"So?" Margery prodded, leaving the word hanging in midair for a long moment after Wulf signaled everyone to attend him in the great hall. "Was the Dane a brute or did he—eh—stir the pot before diving in?"

Gwendolyn blinked, then shuddered at the image.

"I have no wish to speak of my time away." She could not help that her eyes followed him even though she'd told herself he would only break her heart.

Part of her feared he already had.

In spite of herself, she had opened her body to him and in doing so, she'd somehow opened her heart. It was a sly path to a woman's soul, but ever since he'd cut open his hand to prove his gentle intentions toward her, she had felt a growing tenderness for Wulf.

How could she not when he'd treated her so much more kindly than any other man ever had?

"Then you will not mind if I sit beside him at sup?" Margery asked, her voice all veiled sweetness and wicked intent.

At that moment, Gwendolyn recalled her fate was no longer in the earl's hands. Would Gwendolyn reign here as lady? Or would she remain little more than a concubine, succumbing to the heat he stirred within her even as her heart warned her it would lead to more hurt for her. Indeed, given her feelings for Wulf, she wondered if he could end up hurting her worse than Gerald had.

Bruises healed. A broken heart... Well, just look how thoroughly the condition had wounded Wulf.

And heaven help her, didn't her heart already ache every time she thought of him?

"If so much as your *hem* touches the Dane," she warned, turning on Margery and whispering low, "I will show you what the Vikings taught me about the use of an axe."

Just as Wulf had explained to her once, Saxons truly did turn green at the mention of the Dane's weapon of choice. While it was probably crude of her to take some small pleasure in that fact right now, Gwendolyn had the feeling it would be the last pleasure she would know for a long, long time.

Because although Wulf had proposed a practical union between them, he would never offer her what she craved most from him. And what pleasure could there be in his touch, knowing she would never incite the feelings in him that he had in her?

While Margery huffed and puffed her indignation alongside her, Gwen couldn't help but think her days of adventure had landed her right back where she started— under a man's thumb and as much a prisoner as ever.

Only this time, much as she'd like to think otherwise, she'd brought a broken heart along with her.

14

TWO DAYS HAD PASSED since Wulf took over the keep. Gwendolyn knew this well, for she had marked the time on a sundial in her mother's old garden.

She worked there now, taking out her frustrations on an overgrown bed of betony and daisies, foxgloves and hyssop. All around the coastal holding, the Danes labored to implement strategic changes to the walls and battlements, protecting the lands against attack by water—the tactic most likely to be used by Harold's men.

On the first night back home under Wulf's rule, he had not come to her bedchamber after the victory feast, making her think he had only wanted her in the first place to secure his hold on the lands. When she'd seen him briefly the next day, he'd told her that his presence and visibility was extremely important now that he'd claimed the keep—both for her people and for his men. Gwendolyn had understood the plan also worked well for a man attempting to distance himself from her.

From any tenderness he may have felt for her.

She might have dreamed the flicker of connection between them that night before they sailed for the keep.

But she could have sworn something monumental had happened when they'd made love in the wild. And the fact that Wulf seemed to withdraw from her ever since only supported her theory, since his experience with Hedra seemed to have hardened his heart to women for all time. Gwendolyn was frustrated at the unfairness of having to pay the toll for another woman's misdeed.

Then again, Wulf Geirsson could simply be an uncommunicative, hard-hearted Viking who only lusted for wealth and lands, and Gwen had merely imagined the tenderness that night in the wishful regions of her heart.

Spearing a thick ball of roots with a rusted spade, Gwen cursed the rock wall of Dane pride. Did he think he showed weakness to care for another? Or was she deceiving herself that he had ever cared? Perhaps she truly was his temporary diversion—a pleasurable dalliance—for a man who had no intention of ever giving his heart away again.

She was so intent on her labors that the deep voice— now so familiar—caught her off guard.

"Do you wish to uproot all the flowers or just the prettiest ones?"

Dropping her spade, she startled back from where she knelt near the overgrown bed.

Wulf opened the old hazel wattle fence that ringed the garden, the wood creaking with age. He cast a long shadow over the flowers as he neared. Gwendolyn drew off her gloves and dropped them by the spade, but even though she relinquished the gardening tools, she scurried to arm her heart with more subtle weapons.

"It is past time I took up the lady's mantle here." Too late, she realized how that sounded. "Not that I wish to have a place beside you," she hastened to explain. "It's just that the keep has grown dismal in my absence and I would like to take up some of my family's old projects. A valuable library is in disarray. The garden contains plantings from across the continent, yet they are now hidden under hearty native plants strangling the more delicate varieties—"

"I want you to move into the main bedchamber with me." He did not blink as he studied her in the high noon sunlight.

He didn't quite command her. A sennight ago, he would have simply said, *You will move into the main bedchamber.* Of course, he didn't ask her, either.

She swiped a humming bee away from her shoulder, knowing she was as ill-equipped for this conversation as she was to battle the bee. She'd already told him she would not be his concubine.

"I do not think that is wise." Turning from him, she pointed to an empty space on the far side of the garden. "Perhaps when you are done reinforcing the outer walls, you might consider building a loggia there. My mother talked of resurrecting one when they returned from Rome."

Gwen hadn't thought of the loggia or the gardens in a long time. Maybe it had been easier for her not to think about anything that reminded her of her family when she missed them so much. Now, after so much time, she found she wanted to remember them. To honor their lives and what they'd worked to accomplish.

What would they think of her Norse lover?

"Then we must move up our nuptials so you will feel comfortable sharing sleeping quarters." His blue eyes were like the calm sea. Unhurried. Unruffled.

"Nuptials?" Her heart ached to think he would mark this order as some sort of proposal. Was this how a

Dane came to marriage—with no declaration of gentle feelings, but a command to his bed?

"We will wed with all haste now that we have returned to your home." He tucked an arm about her waist and nudged her toward a raised turf-covered bench. "I have won the keep without the help of negotiating a marriage, so I have eased your concern about wedding you for political purposes."

Dropping onto the sun-warmed grass covering the bench, Gwendolyn tried to regroup the scattered defenses of her wayward heart and failed. Wulf truly expected her to be pleased about marrying him, even though he had maneuvered her exactly where he'd wanted her, making her feel as powerless as ever.

Truth be told, part of her wanted to simply agree to the marriage and hope they could come to find happiness together despite the obvious obstacles—his lack of love for her, his impending battle with Harold, a possible claim from Godric for her hand.

Yet how could she ever knowingly place herself in a situation like what she'd experienced with Gerald, where a man came to her bed solely to father children? That the coupling did not hurt her body did not take away the fact that it would steal a piece of her soul every time he left without saying the words she longed to hear.

"I want to choose my next husband." One who wouldn't hurt her body *or* her soul. She did not meet his gaze. Instead, she plucked a dandelion where it grew on the bench beside her. "My last lord suggested I could do as much, but then you arrived and took me away before I was granted that privilege."

Wulf observed the dirt-streaked face of the noblewoman before him, wondering if this was the same female who'd gazed out over the battlements like a queen when he'd landed on her shore less than a fortnight ago. She puttered in the flowers like a gardener, never claiming her rightful place in the great hall, remaining out of sight as much as possible.

Did she hope he would forget her if she eluded his notice? Or had their explosive night together shaken her as much as it had him? Perhaps she sought distance to resurrect control in the same way he had.

That did not mean she could choose her husband. *Thor's hammer.* Did she seek to make every development in their relationship as difficult as possible?

"You wed no one but me." He planned to make that abundantly clear. About this, there would be no misunderstanding. "I have given you more freedom than any captive ever to sail away in a longship. I delayed saying our vows to show you that I choose you freely—with no regard to your political value or wealth."

He waited for her to appreciate the magnitude of this. To recognize how much he touted her worth to him by taking her for no other virtue than that he wanted her.

Yet she scowled at him with thinly disguised fury, her dark brows arcing down like a farmer's plough, her eyes flashing with simmering emotion.

"A woman is not a battle prize." She rose from the bench, scattering the dandelions she had absently yanked from the turf. "I am not an object to which you can assign high value or little. And I am not an ornament for your bed to toy with when you please. No matter that I find pleasure with you or not, my heart wishes to offer more than my womb to my future husband. If all I give you is release in the marriage bed, then I would not be any more useful in this marriage than I was in my last."

Wulf attempted to follow her thinking, but he was

distracted by her abrupt, stomping departure. He had injured her when he meant to honor her.

"Gwendolyn." He held out a hand to her, hoping to understand how to fix it, but she spurned his touch and ran.

The same way she'd run from him the first day he captured her and she'd injured her knee. The same way she'd sought escape by diving off the bow of his ship. And stolen his horse.

Why did he attempt to hold a woman so intent on being free of him? The thought angered him too much for him to chase her just now. He had too many other problems that needed his attention with Harold's army spotted just up the coast.

Besides, it was dangerous to confront a woman when angry. He'd learned to control himself better than that time long ago—when Hedra had chosen to wed Olaf instead of him, the man she claimed to love.

He had been angry, said hurtful things, and probably ensured she did not rethink her choice of the cooler-headed older Geirsson brother. Now, Wulf knew better than to give vent to his hurts. He tried not to have them, of course, but it seemed the fiery Saxon woman was full of surprises.

Although one thing was abundantly clear. She would never wed another. He had that power over her, un-like with Hedra. Just the thought of her with any other man...

His fists clenched at his side. Red-hot fury crawled over his head and burned bright. Muscles tensed and tightened. Spinning on his heel, he punched the nearest object in reach—a tall, weed-choked rose trellis. The rotted wood shuddered and cracked. He yanked his fist back through, the splintered wood raking open his skin as he did so.

"Save it, my friend." A deep voice called to him from the other end of the garden. "You have far more dangerous enemies than the trellis, you know."

Turning, Wulf saw Erik enter the wattle gate to the garden. The last thing Wulf wanted was a lecture on his temper. He swiped the blood from his knuckles onto his tunic and flexed his fist, stinging but not broken.

"I do not need you to tell me who to count among my enemies." Since taking over the Wessex keep, he had heard that Godric—the brother of Gwendolyn's dead husband—had been gathering forces to mount an attack. Wulf knew there were enough foes to go around.

"She is not happy to see you installed as the new lord?" Swiping at loose dirt with his boot, Erik covered the roots of some flowers Gwendolyn had been separating.

A practical and thoughtful gesture that Wulf rather wished he had thought to make. Perhaps his skill with women had vanished long ago.

"She asked me to let her choose her own husband." Wulf was unsure why he admitted as much. But as his family, Erik would not share the tale.

"A bold lady, that one." Erik shook his head and appeared to fight off a grin. "You think she has someone in mind?"

"I will cause him no end of pain if she does," he muttered darkly.

"Perhaps she merely wishes to be given the right, even though she will choose you." Erik handed him the spade and pointed to another clump of hyssop that apparently needed to be thinned while he went about pulling weeds from a thick border of daisies. "I gather

some women do not enjoy being ordered about like oarsmen on a ship."

Wulf dug apart the green stems in question, though
his mind was hardly on the task. He had to prepare to
fight Harold Harraldson and the considerable resources
he would bring to bear on the coastal keep.

Still, as he shook the dirt from a shovel full of roots,
he recalled Gwendolyn's words to him that first day
after he'd taken her.

Leading a woman requires discussion.

"That's it." Wulf recognized the solution to his problem, a practical way to fix the unhappiness Gwendolyn
had been feeling toward him. "I will put the matter in
her hands and let her choose me."

It seemed abundantly clear under the unrelenting rays
of the noontime sun. He needed to give Gwendolyn
some say in her future and trust she would make the
wise decision—the only possible decision. Because like
it or not, Gwendolyn's feelings had become a matter of
importance to him even though he'd promised himself
he would never care deeply about a woman again. As
long as she did not know the power she wielded, all
would be well.

Yet as he stalked from the garden to find her and
make things right, he could not ignore the vague uneasiness that settled over him like a cloud and shadowed his
every step.

COMBING HER DAMP HAIR before the looking glass in
her bedchamber, Gwendolyn thought perhaps she had
overreacted when she walked away from Wulf earlier.

After leaving the garden that afternoon, Gwendolyn
had spent hours in her father's library putting books in
their proper places and reading bits from volumes she

recalled from her childhood. She'd smiled to find the old ink drawing of a Titan, the picture she'd once thought about while gazing upon Wulf.

And as always, the thought of her parents' counsel gave her peace. Patience. Perhaps Wulf had not intended to cut her to the quick with his easy assumption of marriage. He simply did not understand how she carried the hurts of her union with Gerald even now. The thought of being so powerless again—of letting a man dictate her every move—frightened her deeply. The very strength of will in Wulf that she admired, that would keep her people safe, could also make him a difficult man to live with.

Now, drawing a heavy silver comb through her hair to help it dry after her bath, she reminded herself that Wulf was not Gerald. The Dane was a far better man. Because of that, he had far more power to hurt her in ways Gerald could never have. She'd already lost a piece of her heart to him and seen how little he returned her caring.

How deep might the hurt be if she fell all the way in love with the arrogant, infuriating man who had vowed to protect her? Too bad his oath did not safeguard her heart the way it protected the rest of her.

Giving up on drying her hair, Gwen rose from the looking glass to join the others in the great hall. She did not know what her answer to him would be, yet she was determined not to lose her temper again. Or at least, they could set aside their dispute until they both settled down.

She hurried toward the hall for the extra meal. The laborers from the village toiled over the battlements until the sun dipped below the horizon, and Wulf rewarded their efforts by providing a lavish repast after sundown.

The special sup would not last long—another sennight, perhaps. A costly yet clever way to win the hearts of her people.

The Viking had not lied when he said he was wealthy beyond her imaginings.

She departed her bedchamber, savoring the feel of rich fabrics against her clean skin after the days of rough wool and muslin while she traveled with Wulf. The whisper of silk on her thighs called to mind how long it had been since Wulf had visited her bed. Who would have guessed she would miss a man's touch after she'd feared it for so long?

Music from the great hall greeted her ears before she turned the corner into the space. Minstrels from Wulf's temporary encampment to the west had arrived at the keep with the women and children today, transporting the whole of that rough village to her doorstep.

His doorstep. She had to remind herself she was as much a guest at his mercy as anyone.

Turning the corner, she felt the bright torches of the great hall bathe her in warm, golden light. The scent of roasted meat and fresh bread wafted toward her, making her stomach groan appreciatively.

Then she saw him.

Wulf sat in the lord's seat on the dais, a massive ram's horn in one hand and the other draped along the shoulders of Gwen's least favorite widow.

Margery.

Gwendolyn blinked, hoping when she opened her eyes again they would show her a more favorable picture. But she got the exact same view the second time around. The cursed husband-hunter simpered up at him, drooling like a child viewing a sugared fig.

Gwen told herself she had no right to be angry, and

she repeated the lie several times over on her approach to the cozy-looking couple. When she stood there, like a supplicant before the lord on the wrong side of his mighty table, she found she could not hold her tongue.

"My lord." She curtsied prettily, less out of respect than from a need to capture the Dane's attention.

Even through lowered lashes, she could see him remove his arm from her wretched rival's back. The gesture proved small comfort. And by the saints, was that a lump forming in her throat? She would never forgive herself if she shed a tear in front of Margery.

"My lady." He greeted her politely. Warmly. He stood. "We have been holding your seat. We were just discussing—"

"I seek an indulgence," she told him quickly, her eyes still burning with the threat of ridiculous, ill-placed tears. "A favor in exchange for the time I spent as your captive."

He owed her nothing. They both knew as much. Still, she recognized the politics of the moment. He was busy playing the generous lord and would not wish to deny the keep's former lady a favor, especially when his abduction had robbed her of much marital worth.

What man wanted a bride who'd been the sexual plaything of a Dane? Even if he had never laid a finger upon her person, that was the reality of her reputation the moment she'd sailed off in his longship.

Wulf eyed her warily. He knew her well. Beside him, Margery arranged herself prettily on the trestle bench, straightening her posture and leaning subtly close to the man who'd clearly become her new romantic quarry.

"You may ask," he told her, taking his seat again.

The confrontation attracted attention from all around the hall. The minstrels played on, though conversation nearby halted. The villagers pointed their way and whispered behind their hands.

On the other end of the dais, Erik and Elsa watched them closely.

Which was just as well. Wulf would have a more difficult time refusing her in front of so many witnesses. So, in a last ditch effort to save her heart anymore shredding, she made a perfectly reasonable request.

"Because you are not my true overlord, I ask safe passage away from Wessex to King Alfred. He holds the majority of my wealth and will see me wed to my satisfaction, a task better overseen by him than by the man who held me captive."

The collective gasp from the table suggested she'd gone too far. But the cold fury in Wulf's eyes told her in no uncertain terms that she had crossed a line.

It did not surprise her to discover that in wounding him, she felt an echo of the hurt herself. But if he would play so cavalierly with her heart, it was best the battle lines were drawn now. He needed to know where she stood.

She certainly recognized his position when she spied him with the Saxon widow this night.

"You dare too much," he accused, his voice a lethal whisper the entire hall heard.

She did not have time to consider how to argue the point, however, as the guard from the watchtower bellowed from above.

"War ships approach, my lord!"

15

FEMALE SHRIEKS ECHOED up into the high rafters of the great hall. Trestle benches scraped back in unison as the men rose to take up positions on the walls.

Gwendolyn froze. A cold chill spread over her body that had nothing to do with her damp hair.

"You come with me." Wulf's voice vibrated in her ear a split second before his big arm wrapped about her waist and he lifted her against him like a sack of grain.

"I will walk," she protested, trying to wriggle free. "Go lead your men or sharpen your axe or—"

"I will see to your safety first." His grip stayed iron-clad, never relaxing when he climbed steps or pushed through heavy doors.

"I will be safer if you are out there, turning aside an attack." She knew this to be true, yet she worried to think of the consequences. She remembered well that last night at the Dane's village when the women had gifted the men with passionate encounters in case the next day's battle marked their last. Walking away from a fight unscathed was never a given. "I will look to my own safety."

"The last time warships appeared on your shores, you stood on the parapets like a battle prize waiting to be claimed." He changed her position in his arms as they reached a narrow passage leading to the innermost section of the keep. Scooping up her legs, he cradled her against his chest, though he never slowed his pounding stride. "You will not have that opportunity this time since I will deliver you into a guard's hands personally."

His obvious anger with her—over what transpired in the hall or because she'd been too much trouble for him from the day they'd met, she wasn't sure—did not scare off the fears that lodged in her throat as they neared the keep's stronghold.

Women and children ran beside them to take shelter from the oncoming ships. Somewhere below in the courtyard, grindstones scraped and hissed as they sharpened weapons. Men's boots thundered on the ground, ominous warning of the trouble to come.

"I'm sorry I asked to go to the king," Gwendolyn whispered, her voice diminished because of the breathless panic that swamped her for Wulf's sake. He was a brilliant warrior—she knew this. Yet managing a keep came new to him. He usually fought from the water, raiding and leaving with deadly swiftness. How would he fare on the other side of such an attack?

"You show a warrior's skill at finding a man's vulnerable parts and slicing deeply." He tossed off the comment in anger, his hard footsteps jostling her as he maneuvered through the crush of people to deliver her to the safety of the innermost sanctum—the secure central tower keep at the heart of the structure.

Did he really mean those words? Did he believe she held any power to hurt him?

Regret nipped hard.

"I was wounded to see Margery held close to your chest like your newest conquest." She lowered her voice as they entered the high stone chamber, windowless save the light-giving open roof many feet overhead. Wooden rafters there provided small protection against the rain.

"The cloying widow? I could not hear her voice, which is thin as a child's. I had to rope her closer just to decipher that she found the mead too strong." Wulf set Gwendolyn on her feet in front of one of his guards—a thickset man he introduced as Osbert. "You will remain here until I retrieve you personally. Do you understand?"

She still reeled from the news that she'd behaved like a foolish, lovesick maid to confront Wulf so rashly in the hall. Nay. More than that, she staggered from his remark that she had wounded him. What woman could wound a man lest he cared a bit for her?

"Yes." Nodding, she planned to agree with whatever he said. She only prayed she would have the chance to make this right with him after a victorious end to the battle. "I will not move until you come for me. May your gods and mine fight on your side."

Arching up on her toes, she kissed his jaw, which was as high as she could reach without some aid from him. He peered down at her strangely, as if he did not understand her at all.

By the saints, she'd made a mess of things with him. In protecting herself, she'd behaved no better than the last woman who had trifled with his heart—and left him with a wound he still carried.

"Aye." He nodded, a terse gesture that revealed nothing. His blue eyes were like the sea before the storm, churning uneasily with cloudy color. "We will discuss your options for marriage afterward."

With that, he turned on his heel and left, effectively dumping her in the holding cell for women and babes. Pandemonium reigned as tears flowed from worried mothers and wives. Osbert and the other two Danes charged with guarding them appeared unmoved, their gazes turned away from the chaos to monitor the sole entrance to the structure.

She watched Wulf's broad shoulders turn sideways through the door to fit through the stream of villagers' wives and kitchen staff now joining the ladies and children in the keep. Gwendolyn fought the temptation to chase down the Dane for another kiss, but hadn't she sworn to stay put? Ignoring the lure of what Wulf would call her "passionate nature," she remained dutifully inside the keep though she hated knowing she would be ignorant of what went on outside the gray walls.

She had a bad feeling about the battle, an uneasiness in her gut that she struggled to ignore. Perhaps she was merely upset about the words she'd exchanged with Wulf in the hall after she'd vowed to keep her temper.

Taking a seat on the floor beside the baker's wife and young daughter, Gwendolyn offered to hold the baby to give the mother's arms a rest. Everyone suffered from overheating after the scramble of running to the innermost keep. Fear added another sticky element to the packed bodies.

At least when Margery came in, she sat on the opposite wall. Though Gwen noticed she'd lingered at the doorway bidding farewell to a man Gwen did not recognize. Just how many prospective husbands did she have?

With an effort, Gwendolyn ignored her and the pit

of anxiety churning through her belly to focus on the shred of hope she'd savored from her conversation with Wulf. He'd given her reason to believe he had a heart beneath the warrior armor.

That alone would ensure she played the role he wanted for her in this battle. Captive no more, Gwen found she was more bound to the Dane than ever.

THE BATTLE DID NOT FEEL RIGHT from the beginning.

Wulf swung his sword with a wide, wild arc as he repelled Harold's men on the battlements. Sweat stung his eyes and blood from a cut on his head distracted him, hampering his vision when he needed to see clearly. He did not tire; nay, he welcomed the chance to finally meet Harold's vengeance with a year's worth of frustrations. But something bothered him about the encounter.

Harold's men fought like they wanted to conquer the keep, not just win Wulf's head on a pike. They mounted ladders to scramble over the walls, attempts that so far had been foiled by Wulf's men. But if even a few of Harold's warriors succeeded, would the Saxon villagers recognize one Dane from another? What havoc might Harold's men wreak within the walls if they were mistaken for Wulf's people?

Dispatching his latest opponent, Wulf reached to push the newest wooden ladder aside from the walls. An arrow stung his hand, landing in the narrow space between his thumb and forefinger to stick between the rocks of the parapets.

Odin's beard.

Desperation tinged the air in ways he had not expected. The loss of life on both sides would be detrimental to all. Could Harold not see that? Had he ceased to be an effective leader?

Swiping away more blood and sweat, Wulf turned from the shouts and oaths of the men who rode the falling ladder backward to the ground. He moved down the battlements to another area at risk for climbing Danes when Erik appeared at his elbow.

"Wulf, the watchtower guards say there are attackers by land on the other side." Erik's sword arm hung awkwardly at his side, though that hand now clutched his axe. His sword he brandished with the less dominant arm. "There is some talk it could be a troop raised by Godric to take Lady Gwendolyn. Perhaps he made an alliance with Harold—"

"Go to the keep where the women are locked up." Everything rattled inside at the thought of harm coming to Gwendolyn. "You are worth ten of Osbert and I need to be sure they are safe." He had not wanted to leave a Saxon in charge of the women, but with his own forces so thin to defend the large keep, he had no choice.

"I can still fight," Erik argued, his shoulders tense for battle. "Do not banish me into the keep for an injury that is less than naught—"

"I send you because I will unleash the wrath of the Christians' hell if any harm comes to Gwendolyn, do you understand?" He started running, passing men in the heat of battle, clubbing two enemies seeking a foothold on the parapet.

She'd kissed him before he left her, and he had not even returned the gesture. No wonder the world thought him a barbarian. Would he commit the same mistake again—to care for a woman and horde the sensation for the sake of pride? He had not forgiven the wound Hedra had inflicted when she wed Olaf and they had both paid a terrible price for it. Could he be so blind and stubborn again to hurt Gwendolyn when he prized her so dearly his chest ached at the thought of Godric getting his hands on her?

He tore up one staircase and down another to reach the battlements on the far side of the keep. Only a few guards—Saxon villagers who had been willing to swear an oath of loyalty—were still here, the vast majority of his manpower having been assigned to fight the battle in progress to the south end of the structure. These men were huddled together in deep conversation, their attention trained over the lands to the north.

"What news?" Wulf could already see the riders at the woods' edge, a war party that could be fifty men or hundreds, depending what was hidden beyond the tree line.

"We saw activity there early this morn," one of the men began, his eyes shifting to his companions as if to validate his story. "But they were obviously Saxons and we did not think they were a threat."

Were they so stupid? Or had he been betrayed from within that the guards had not alerted him earlier?

"The first few were not dressed for war," one of the others clarified, his gaze equally shifty while his hands alternately clenched and flexed around his crossbow. "We thought it a traveling party, or a group that might approach to seek shelter."

That one was nervous, Wulf decided, though whether it was about his incompetence or for his backstabbing treachery, he could not be certain.

"You do not decide what warrants my attention. If a rabbit pisses within a stone's throw of these walls, I hear about it." Wulf picked up the nearest man by the collar and yanked him up to eye level. "If you have betrayed me, your life is already forfeit."

These Saxons could have previously slipped someone

inside the gates, taking advantage of Harold's invasion. Which meant Gwendolyn could already be in danger.

Dropping the man unceremoniously to the ground, Wulf vowed to replace every Saxon in sight with a Dane loyal to him and no other. He would not risk Gwendolyn's safety in the hands of more beef-witted louts and gold-seeking schemers.

He just prayed he wasn't too late to save her from the enemies converging upon them on all sides.

THE EERIE QUIET OF THE CROWDED chamber unnerved her.

Gwendolyn sat among more than a hundred women and children, yet except for the fitful cry of one tired babe, no one made a sound. As one, the group strained to gauge the battle outside by the din of clanking steel weaponry, the shouts of the commanders and the harrowing gurgles and moans of the dying. Could each woman distinguish the sound of her man's voice?

Heaven knew Gwendolyn could differentiate Wulf's voice from any other. She longed to hear it now, any sign that he yet lived precious beyond bearing.

For her part, Gwendolyn had rocked her small charge to sleep soon after they'd been secured inside the keep and now she handed the snoozing child back to her mother's arms. She did not know how she would withstand the idle hours of waiting, but she prayed this battle would win Wulf peace for many years. A strong warrior deterred enemies by reputation alone and once Wulf turned back Harold, Gwendolyn could not imagine any other would dare approach this keep while he ruled.

Now, while Osbert eyed the door with a watchful intensity that would freeze any intruders in their tracks, Margery rose from her place along the far wall to offer

one of the other guards a drink from the well that ran
beneath the structure. Between the fresh water supply
and the permanent food stores maintained here, people
could take shelter in the keep for weeks if necessary. The
thought of being shut in for so long made her shudder.

It was while Margery flirted with the guard and made
a show of giving him some water that the bar on the
entrance shifted. Could it be news from the battle?

"Open up, Osbert." A muffled voice sounded through
the door. "'Tis Erik. Wulf wants me to assist you."

Gwendolyn would not have heard the exchange if she
had not been seated so close to the guard—just where
Wulf had put her. She thought Erik's request strange, but
then the battle sounded worse—and closer—than what
she'd imagined. Perhaps it did not go well for Wulf's
men.

"You guard the door from without. I will remain
within," Osbert said reasonably, his brow thick with
sweat though he had done no more than safeguard the
door these last hours.

In the meantime, Margery wove her way through the
crowded keep to offer another drink to a second man-
at-arms. Did the woman have to throw herself at every
male old enough to wield a sword?

"Treachery is afoot," Erik shouted from the other side
of the door. "Wulf would have me guard his lady."

The claim must have sounded as plausible to Osbert
as it did to Gwendolyn, for he reached to open the door
with one hand while waving forward his men with the
other as back-up.

Two of them did not respond with any speed, their
steps slow and unsteady as if they'd spent the day swill-
ing strong mead. It was the same two men for whom

Margery had just fetched water. Could the drink have been tainted?

Or could Margery have tampered with it?

Treachery is afoot.

But by the time Gwendolyn shouted a warning to Osbert, it was too late. He'd unlatched the door.

Snarling Saxon raiders poured into the stronghold with swords drawn and helms masking their features. Erik was nowhere in sight. Osbert fought valiantly, yet fell quickly, as did the only other guard still standing. The befuddled two who'd consumed something tainted did not even have their swords drawn when they were cut down.

Beside her, the baker's wife screamed and clung to her leg. The invaders did not hurt the women, they merely stood guard over them the way the Danes had mere moments ago. All except the man that faced her.

As he tugged off the helm with an ugly boar's head draped over top of it, Gwendolyn glimpsed a face even more awful.

Godric, her dead husband's brother, had come to claim her.

16

CAPTIVITY WITH GODRIC bore no resemblance to Gwendolyn's abduction by Wulf.

In her mind, Gwen relived those happier days in the woods with Wulf while Godric and his men bound her hands and hobbled her feet before leading her out of the central keep. The rough rope shredded her skin as they yanked it tight. A coarse wool cloth stank of sweat when they gagged her. Stomach roiling in protest as she stumbled down a step, she tried to hear the sounds of the nearby battle for some hint of how Wulf fared. Did he win the day? Would he notice her missing soon, or would he be too engrossed in the fighting to discover she'd been taken?

Her scalp stung where one of Godric's men had yanked out a bit of hair while tying her gag. She guessed she had been taken from the inner keep into the small, rear courtyard, but she'd been blindfolded so she could not be sure. The usual landmarks around the keep were hidden behind catapults and extra horses. Everything felt different around her home since the Danes arrived.

Since Wulf brought her back.

Her heart ached for him as her captors pushed and

shoved her along despite her tripping, awkward pace. Finally, the men shrouded her in a blanket like a corpse. Even her head was covered. There was no concern for her shoes getting wet or her knee becoming injured when they slung her body over a man's shoulder and— moments later—over a horse's back. They would surely kill her while transporting her if this spoke of their level of care. The one bright spot in that would be the errant bastards would never see a farthing of her fabled dowry if she did not make the trip alive.

How could these traitors hide what they did in a keep held by Danes? Was there no one loyal to Wulf to spot this hasty retreat from the inner keep? Perhaps all the battle remained to the south. She supposed that could account for the knaves' ease in removing her from the central tower.

In low voices, she heard men discussing which exit to use from the keep. Someone must have helped these Saxons enter from the inside. She guessed Alchere had left behind more supporters than Wulf had guessed, and she kicked herself for not becoming more involved in his questioning of the men who remained. Would she have been able to spot those who would not be loyal to him?

Or was the widow Margery the only enemy from within? Gwendolyn had known all along she was trouble. Just not how much.

Blinking away tears of frustration, fear and pain, Gwen feared she would never see Wulf again if Godric succeeded in removing her from the castle. Why hadn't she wed him when she had the chance? Would that have prevented Godric from taking her? Now, she would never get to tell Wulf that she didn't need a declaration of undying love to be his wife. That she understood a man of few words didn't necessarily equal a man of few emotions. That she loved him.

Her certainty of that fact made her all the more determined to escape Godric. She could not allow Wulf to return from battle only to find another woman had disappeared or—she inhaled a steadying breath—died. Heaven knew, Godric's men did not treat her like an intended bride. Perhaps he only stole Gwen in revenge against Wulf for besting him a sennight ago.

A heavy rider climbed on the animal near her. She tried frantically to clutch the horse's sides when the man whipped the beast's flank to get it moving, but with her hands tied, the best she could do was steady herself with her elbows. At least they did not move very fast. Judging by the slower, halting way it moved, the animal was a donkey. A plaintive bray quickly confirmed her suspicions. Did that mean she stood a better chance of not cracking open her head if she chose to roll off its back on purpose?

Because no way in Hades would she depart her home if she had any strength left in her body to fight. She'd nearly escaped the strongest warrior in Christendom on two different occasions; she would not be bested by a brigand bastard like Godric.

Before she could determine the best direction to heave herself off the animal, however, she heard a familiar voice thick with the accent of the Danes.

"Someone here knows where she is." The unleashed fury in Wulf's raised voice stoked hope inside her. "And if I do not start hearing answers right now, you will lose your chance to tell me forever since I will ask Erik to hack out your tongues with his axe."

Gwendolyn closed her eyes under the woolen blanket and let the mixture of relief and fear wash through her.

Wulf could not see her. So while it helped to know he was near, he had not yet discovered her hiding place on the back of a donkey.

And by the sounds of it, the scene was about to become a gruesome one if she didn't act fast. Godric's tongue could go, but she rather hoped Wulf would not follow through on the threat with anyone else.

"Mmpf!" She struggled against the donkey, lifting her chest the little bit she could with her elbows pressed to the animal's side.

It was more difficult than expected to move. Still, she wriggled and yelled behind the gag.

"My lord," a Saxon voice called out.

Had someone seen her movements?

"Thor's hammer." Wulf shouted the oath as if he expected his god to come down with that particular weapon aimed at the enemy's head.

In no time, she felt the silent slide of the rider's body next to her as he slumped off the animal to the ground. Huge, blessedly familiar hands lifted her from the haunches, cradling her tenderly. She wanted to smile, knowing who held her, but the twine on her gag bit into the corners of her mouth.

"I've got you." The gentleness in his voice—so different than his threat to tear out tongues—was further proof of caring from a warrior who had little to say but would go to any lengths to back up what words he did choose.

He walked a short distance as, around them, the sounds of battle grew more muted. Could Wulf have routed Harold even as he saved her from Godric?

"Gwendolyn?" He tugged at the blanket, but could not unwind the tight material enough to free her without setting her down.

"Clear the bench," he ordered, and she heard metal clank as bodies hurried to do his bidding. More quietly, he spoke just above her ear. "I will never rest until the men who hurt you pay."

They were not gentle words, but she understood now that this promise—like the blood oath he'd once made her—was his way of showing her he cared. She had not lost her heart to a man like her father who'd devoted his life to books and words. She'd fallen for a warrior.

Tenderly, he laid her down on the turf bench and she knew by the soft grass under her back that they were in her mother's garden. The battle must have spread all over the holding.

Finally, the smothering blanket eased. Sunlight warmed her face and made her blink. She heard Wulf cursing before she distinguished his face in the slanted light of the setting sun.

"For the love of Freya, Erik," he shouted. "Use a smaller knife to cut those bonds. That is my woman's flesh beneath the rope, not a hare in a trap."

Wulf's hands went to the gag around her mouth while others sawed away at the ties on her hands and feet. She attempted to remain very, very still, her eyes never leaving Wulf's face.

Thank God he was unhurt, though by the rood, he'd been spattered in enough blood to make him appear every inch the terrifying savage.

"Are you hurt?" Wulf spoke softly to her, his big body crowding her on the bench. He eased away the gag and called for water.

She settled for shaking her head as she discovered her mouth would not work. Her toes and hands tingled painfully to life as they experienced the flow of blood again.

All her bonds were free. Her hands shook as she reached for the cup of water that someone brought. Wulf helped Gwendolyn to sit and steadied the vessel for her even as he supported her shoulders. The cool water revived her before she recalled the well might have been tainted.

"Have we won?" she asked, disoriented that so many of Wulf's men stood about her when there were still sounds of battle in the distance.

"Spoken like a Dane." Wulf smoothed her hair from her face.

Wincing, she felt the sting of the raw patch on her scalp where one of the brutes had wrenched out her hair.

Wulf frowned as he examined the injury more closely. Erik approached with a wet cloth that Wulf took from his hands to smooth over Gwendolyn's face.

"The battle is mostly won," Wulf confided, his blue eyes halting on each scratch he discovered. "Godric's men met Alchere's and formed an alliance to attack the same day as Harold. But since the Saxons cannot tell a Norseman from a Dane, let alone one Dane from another, they ended up inflicting more harm on Harold's men that mine."

"Serves them all right," she muttered darkly.

"After we send them on their way, none of them will ever return," Wulf vowed, his hand stalling just above the corner of her mouth where she knew a fresh cut bled.

Why was it the smallest scrapes hurt most of all?

"After you send them on their way, I have much to tell you," she confided, taking the cloth from his hands to tend the small wound herself. "I love—"

"My lord!" a man's voice boomed through the small

rear courtyard, cutting off the most significant declaration of her life.

Wulf shot to his feet, shoulders tense.

Scant feet away, a Saxon knight held a chained Dane that Gwendolyn had never seen before. The man's shoulders spanned nearly as great a width as Wulf's and his bloodied and mud-spattered garments were heavy with patches of fur and metalwork. Over his chain mail hung a silver brooch outlined in vivid blue stones that must have come from a far-off land. His helm listed to one side as he limped, but the horns on either side of the headpiece had to have come from the biggest boar any man had ever killed.

"Harold." Wulf's pronouncement confirmed Gwendolyn's only guess.

"One of your men captured him in battle, but asked me to bring him to you." The Saxon knight did not sheathe the sword he'd used to prod along the Dane, and he appeared grateful to hand off his sizable prisoner to Erik.

Gwendolyn held her breath, not knowing what to expect. Would the two warriors battle to the death here? Now? Had she dodged captivity with Godric only to see Wulf cut down or forced to kill a grieving man? Both options were impossible. Both outcomes too horrible to contemplate.

Not sure what else to do, she reached for the only part of Wulf close enough to touch—his hand—and squeezed.

WULF HAD NEVER FELT the silent, empathetic touch of a woman so close to a battle.

That wordless brush of her fingers said more to him than any conversation could have, and he appreciated the humanizing connection at a moment when he wanted every enemy to fall to his knees. Arriving at the inner tower to find his men struck down and her gone, all he had thought of was the wise woman's warning that he would pay a grave price to defeat Harold. Seeing Gwendolyn wrapped up like a dead body had hacked more years off his life than any encounter with a skilled opponent. Fury flamed hot at all those who played any role in bringing her to harm. Harold had conspired with the Saxons to attack him from all sides, hadn't he? By rights this king should be groveling for his life.

Yet Gwendolyn's steady touch—those soft but strong hands that opened him up to a world of feelings beyond any he'd imagined—helped Wulf to see the aging ruler behind the fierce helm. To see the man who'd lost someone he loved.

"Are you ready to pay homage to me and put this feud behind us?" Wulf asked, his hand coming to rest on his sword.

"You have turned into a war machine," Harold declared, rattling his chained hands as if to remind Wulf he had not been freed to fight. "You rebuffed the combined efforts of three enemies between the course of one sunrise and one sunset."

"That is not an answer, old man," Wulf taunted, refusing to lose focus. He did not think for a moment that Harold respected his war-mongering skills or the stubborn Dane would not have launched a campaign at so great a cost.

"I would gladly give my life to avenge Hedra. But if I win, I take your Saxon prize for a keepsake." The warrior cast lustful eyes on Gwendolyn and it was all Wulf could do not to end it then and there—even with his enemy's hands chained.

"Do you bait me in the hope I end your life quickly?" He would not allow Gwendolyn to further be harmed.

"Do I bait you?" Harold lifted a shaggy blond eyebrow that had long ago been bisected by an enemy's blade. "I thought I merely bartered terms."

Wulf said nothing, unwilling to discuss Gwendolyn with his enemy. Perhaps if he kept Harold talking, the battle would be won decisively and there would be naught to do but send him back to Daneland on one of his ships.

All Wulf wanted was to carry Gwendolyn to his bed and tend her wounds. Care for her until she understood there would never be anyone else for him but her.

"I have never known the hard-hearted Wulf Geirsson to admit such weakness for a female," Harold pressed, watching Wulf like a hawk as though it was he who stood in chains and Harold who had all the power here.

All around them, Wulf's men gave them room to fight if they chose, while Erik held Harold's sword and the key to the man's manacles.

"She is not your concern." Wulf wanted the discussion over and Harold gone. He gave the sign to Erik to free his enemy so the battle could begin. "You may have your sword if you wish to claim vengeance, but you will not look upon my woman again."

Despite a grievously wounded leg and a legion of men lost, Harold Haaraldson stretched his mouth in what could only be a grin.

"Nay. I will not look upon her. And I will pay homage to you on your lands. If you allow me to go, I will accept the wergild you paid for Hedra and leave you in peace."

Behind Wulf, Gwendolyn gasped. Once again, her

gentle hand brushed his arm. And to Wulf's surprise, he felt unsteady enough that he needed to reach back and hold on to her hand, as well.

"What trick is this?" He saw Erik step away from the king and knew Harold could take his sword anytime, but he did not move for it.

"No trick." Harold waved the sword and Erik aside. "Anger has eaten away at me all year, Wulf. Not just because of Hedra, but because I did not believe you mourned her enough or even loved her the way the misguided girl adored you."

Wulf had taken sword blows that stung less than that accusation.

"You have no right to judge—"

"Perhaps not." Harold raised a hand to cut him off. "Either way, I can see now that you are not just a warrior. And now—finally—I can believe that maybe Hedra wounded you as much as you hurt her. Because with my own eyes, I see that you are capable of losing your heart just like any other mortal man. For me, that is enough justice for my sister."

The older man had the gall—nay, the iron-clad balls—to turn his back on Wulf and head for the garden gate even though he stood in a thicket of Saxons and enemy Danes.

Beside him, Gwendolyn squeezed his arm. "Say something," she urged, her quick-witted tongue always finding words faster.

Releasing the hilt of his sword Wulf called to him.

"Where do you think you are going?" He gestured to the thick walls of the fortress all around the courtyard.

"I am returning to my ships and giving the order to retreat." Harold turned, holding his weight off his wounded leg. "We will not see one another again in this lifetime, Wulf. You do not need to fear me."

He really intended to just sail home. End of story. All because he thought Wulf had a heart and that he'd lost it.

A cagey opponent, Harold Haaraldson.

Not having the same facility with words as his Saxon lady, Wulf settled for pounding his chest with his fist. It was an old gesture of respect for the Danes.

His men followed suit, the crash of hard knuckles on chainmail filling the courtyard.

Harold closed his hand and repeated the gesture once. Twice. Then he raised his fist as if to rally his army, and stalked off toward the battlements, the setting sun streaking his departure with bright gold and purple.

An old weight rolled off Wulf's shoulders. He hadn't realized how the dark the cloud over him had been until just now when he felt the last of the day's light on his shoulders and saw Gwendolyn peer up at him with misty eyes.

"He must be a good king," she announced in the hush of the aftermath.

Erik waved the others out of the garden although he remained to stand guard. A good man, that one.

"He has always been a strong leader," Wulf agreed, waiting to pull her closer until he saw some sign from her, some sense of how she felt about their future. "You understand now why I did not wish to kill him."

Gwendolyn gave him a small smile, clearly careful of the cuts about her mouth. All Wulf could think of was how grateful he was to have her back. Safe. His.

Or so he fervently hoped. He could have tolerated any defeat today save losing this woman who meant everything to him.

"Does it hurt overmuch?" He lifted her in his arms, not giving her the option of walking.

Gwendolyn did not know it yet, but he did not plan to let her leave his chamber for a fortnight at least. His heart—a very real organ he possessed despite commonly held rumor—would not tolerate another scare like today.

"I am well enough," she assured him, tipping her head close to his chest.

"Excellent." Heedless of the destruction about them, and Godric and the rest of the Saxon prisoners being led to a holding area, Wulf strode toward the living area behind the outer bailey. Toward his chamber. "I know a priest who will be glad to attend you in our chamber if you are able to speak the vows."

GWENDOLYN SWALLOWED HARD.

This was what she wanted. And she'd told herself that she did not mind if Wulf did not always speak the words she wanted to hear. She really believed that. But by the saints, could he not mark the occasion with a few tender sentiments?

Nay. But she would.

"Wulf." She placed her hand on his chest as he ducked into a narrow entrance to the gallery over the living quarters. "I cannot wait to be your wife."

His pace slowed from a hard charge to a thoughtful walk.

"I cannot wait another moment for you to be mine." The heat in his voice reminded her of that night together outside his encampment when they'd talked about how passion fueled the lives of his people.

Her heart warmed at his declaration. Simple. Direct. Heartfelt.

She knew it in her bones.

"But since it is a momentous occasion, could we not wash away the blood of the day first?"

Wulf paused outside his bedchamber, his face shadowed in the harsh light of flickering torches. At first, he frowned. Then, after a moment, he threw back his dark head and laughed.

"Yes." He kicked open the door to his chamber. "By all that is holy, we will wash this day from our skin first. I need hot water," he called out into the empty corridor like a man accustomed to having his wishes granted. "And a tub."

"I fear no one is here to serve you. They are all out wading through the wreckage." Gwendolyn hated to think of so much destruction. So much to rebuild.

"After a battle, everyone wants to return to normal. Even if there is no meal, they gather in the hall because it is familiar." He settled her on his bed and then moved back to the door.

A knock sounded upon it before he even reached it.

"You see?" He swung it wide with a flourish, and sure enough, most every child that resided in the village stood outside the door with a bucket in hand.

Gwendolyn recognized several of them from those quiet, awful hours locked up in the keep. She gave thanks the day had been won and all of them had remained safe.

One by one, they trooped in to fill a tub carried by the biggest of them—a boy almost old enough that he could have fought with a sword this day. Another year, and he would be among the men.

In no time, the water was poured, dried rose petals thrust in by a small, giggling girl at the end of the line, and the group shuffled out of the chamber to whatever repast the cooks offered in the hall. Gwendolyn had no doubt that Wulf would use his ample resources to be sure the widows were housed and all his people fed. But for tonight—right now—she had this magnificent man all to herself.

"Would you like assistance?" Wulf asked, locking the door behind the children and approaching the bed.

The low rumble of his voice told her he thought about the same things that she did. Removing their clothes. Being together.

In spite of the dark hell wrought today, her body warmed in anticipation.

"I think if I have help, I will not end up in the tub." She smiled shyly at him, remembering how scared she had been of his touch a week ago.

So much had changed. She had changed.

"I would take another oath—"

"Nay!" Shaking her head, she tugged her smock up and off. "It was only a manner of speaking. I trust you."

His avid gaze raked over her body in her thin shift and a blush crawled over her skin.

"You must speak less, perhaps?" He did not quite suppress his teasing smile.

"No. This, I will not do." Making quick work of the shift, she dashed for the tub and dropped into the water with a squeal. "The water is scarcely warmer than the river."

"Then I will warm you." He stripped off his tunic and belt, his weapons hitting the floor with a clank of steel against stone.

She licked her lips at the sight he made. A few dark bruises shadowed some places, but his hardened male strength had kept him alive and safe. Her valiant warrior. Her favorite captor.

"I cannot imagine how you will fit." The oval basin was deep, but narrow.

"Women like to say that, but it has never been the case." He strode over to the tub and stepped inside, lifting her easily to sit on his lap.

"You are wicked," she accused, breathless from the feel of his naked thighs beneath her rump. "But before we, ah…consummate the marriage that will happen sooner or later, I have things I would like to say to you."

Reaching for a rag and soap on a bench near the foot of his bed, Wulf soaked the linen and began to wash her face with gentle strokes.

"That is good, because I did not really mean you should talk less. I like all the things you have to say. You could be a scholar, like your father."

Her eyes burned with tears.

"That is the kindest thing anyone has said to me in…a very long time."

Wulf tipped up her chin, studying her face as if curious to see the emotions she couldn't contain.

"I will take good care of you and tell you more kind things." His utter seriousness stole her heart for keeps.

She took the wet linen from him and cleaned away the blood over his eye.

"I love you, Wulf." She realized she hadn't spoken those words since her parents rode off without her many summers ago. "I know you believe in living with passion more than speaking about it, but it is important to me that you know my heart is yours. And I have faith that no wise woman can see the future as well as I do, because I am certain I can make you happy as no other ever could."

"Gwendolyn." Tenderly, he pried the wash rag from her hands and shifted her in the tub so she faced him. "From the first, I told you that I would never wed a woman unless I wished to touch no one but her for the rest of my days. I have found that woman in you."

Gwendolyn launched herself at him, flinging wet arms around his neck, squeezing him for dear life.

"That is so good. So wonderful. Because I will never let you go and I will never share you." Her cut wrists stung where she clasped them together behind his neck, but she did not care. He had told her the words her heart longed to hear.

And by God, she knew he meant them.

"I love you, Gwendolyn." He whispered it softly, into her damp hair. "Even Harold knew it. I did not understand it at first, but I had to have you the moment I saw you standing on the battlements, your veils whipping around you like a foreign princess."

She kissed his neck and his shoulder, easing back to revel in his words and the devotion of a man she trusted to keep her heart safe.

"My feet must have been drawn up those stairs for a reason." She had been destined to meet Wulf, to be his wife.

"Aye." He splayed a hand along her back and pressed her tight to him. "You were meant to be my captive. And I was meant to be yours."

Epilogue

Seven months later

"IF I HAVE TO EAT ONE more fig, I will throw off all my clothes and start dancing naked like the maiden in the work of art you've been admiring over the hearth."

Gwendolyn made the threat lightly as she rubbed her flat belly and teased the overprotective warrior seated at the table beside her. They dined in a grand palazzo of Venice in a far-flung corner of the kingdom of Italy. One of many stops on a tour by sea that had delighted Gwendolyn for the past many months.

They'd traveled to Brittany and Bordeaux, hugging the coastline of Francia and then the kingdom of Asturias and Leon to visit Santiago de Compostela. Finally, they'd sailed into the blue, blue waters of the Mediterranean to see Barcelona and Rome, in honor of her parents. They'd crossed Italy by land to see Venice before they began the trek home.

After securing the keep, Wulf had offered her an adventure and she had thrived on every moment of discovery. New worlds had opened her mind and her heart until she felt full to overflowing with life, love and happiness.

And just now, figs.

"You will maintain your strength," he commanded, though he changed strategies by handing her a plump grape from a heavy silver platter instead. "My child will not be a puny Saxon, but a Dane to be reckoned with. You must nourish the babe with this in mind. But if you are of a mind to strip off your clothing to prove a point, you will witness how fast I can have you upstairs and underneath me."

Warming at his stare, Gwendolyn could not believe how delicious it felt to love and be loved by her husband. She had only been sure she was expecting for about a fortnight, but Wulf already treated her as if she carried a full-grown babe.

They had wed the morning after the battle with Harold since they had found ways to pleasure each other despite their injuries. With Goderic dead and Alchere fled to one of his holdings, Wulf and Gwendolyn had celebrated their nuptials. Elsa and Erik had witnessed the nuptials and the keep celebrated with feasting for a fortnight. They had timed the ceremony to coincide with King Alfred's return. And while the Saxon king was not pleased to have a Dane in charge at a Wessex keep, he was swayed by the feasting and the news he'd received of Wulf's resounding defeat of all comers. Besides, as a wedding present to Gwendolyn, Wulf had declared fealty to the king of his new homeland.

"You must wait," she pleaded sweetly, knowing how fast Wulf Geirsson could deliver on a promise. "You said we could visit the countess's library and bribe her into selling us a book."

Part of the reason they'd made their journey—besides the adventure—was so that Gwendolyn could add to her parents' library collection. She did not have the same ambition to be a scholar as her father, but she hoped to open the keep to visitors again, to bring the world to her door during the years when she would not want to travel. Once the baby arrived, she would be very content to stay home.

"We do not have enough manuscripts already?" Wulf downed his wine and seemed not to notice the hungry glances from the lady diners in the sun-drenched palazzo's hall. He drew feminine eyes wherever he went, but true to his word, he never showed the slightest inclination to admire other women. "I will be fortunate to pay for our return trip home if you find many more volumes."

He offered to buy her jewels and silks, furs and metalwork everywhere they visited. But she'd been steadfast in her wishes. Although there had been a lovely glass hanging lamp on an island called Murano that she couldn't resist.

"Do not be cross. You made a small fortune from ransoming Margery and the others back to Alchere and we agreed we would spend every farthing that foul woman brought in."

"True. But you realize we could acquire more books if I went raiding for them?" He rose and took her hand to help her to her feet.

"You have reformed, remember?" She tucked her arm in his as he led her over the bright marble floors and out into the sunshine. "And we agreed this would be our last book before we return home. Will you miss Venice and all our travels?"

Gwen loved the way the warm air swirled in off the water of this magical city. Still, she found she missed her mother's garden a bit. And she had grown fond of Elsa's surly practicality. She had not been afraid to wade into the village after the wedding celebration and help the women set their homes to right. Gwendolyn enjoyed her ease with getting her hands dirty despite her noble status.

"Now that there is the babe to consider, I will be glad to return home." Wulf stepped off the street into the small boat he'd commissioned for their stay in this city on the water. "I want to know you are both well protected and close to the midwife."

"You won't miss adventuring?" She took his hand as he helped her down into the vessel that was not half the watercraft as his longship. Gwendolyn had been well educated during the voyage on what made the Danes' ships superior to any in the world.

"Did you forget I spent the whole year on the sea before we met? I will not mind sitting still for a little while. I will have your king send me noble Saxon sons to foster and I can teach them to fight like real men." He pounded his chest, mostly because he knew it made her smile. "Besides, I married the adventure. I cannot possibly leave it behind."

Gwendolyn stretched out on her seat in the sun-warmed boat, happy to watch her husband's strong arms flex as he steered her wherever they wanted to go.

"I think Italy agrees with you, my lord. You're developing quite a way with words."

The heat returned to his blue gaze and he dropped the oars at once. With the balance of a man who'd spent his life on the sea, he bracketed her hips with his arms and covered her mouth with his.

And for the next hour, tucked in the cramped cabin draped in silks at the back of the boat, no words were needed.

* * * * *

Harlequin Intrigue top author
Delores Fossen presents
a brand-new series of breathtaking
romantic suspense!
TEXAS MATERNITY: HOSTAGES
The first installment available May 2010:
THE BABY'S GUARDIAN

Shaw cursed and hooked his arm around Sabrina.

Despite the urgency that the deadly gunfire created, he tried to be careful with her, and he took the brunt of the fall when he pulled her to the ground. His shoulder hit hard, but he held on tight to his gun so that it wouldn't be jarred from his hand.

Shaw didn't stop there. He crawled over Sabrina, sheltering her pregnant belly with his body, and he came up ready to return fire.

This was obviously a situation he'd wanted to avoid at all cost. He didn't want his baby in the middle of a fight with these armed fugitives, but when they fired that shot, they'd left him no choice. Now, the trick was to get Sabrina safely out of there.

"Get down," someone on the SWAT team yelled from the roof of the adjacent building.

Shaw did. He dropped lower, covering Sabrina as best he could.

There was another shot, but this one came from a rifleman on the SWAT team. Shaw didn't look up, but he heard the sound of glass being blown apart.

The shots continued, all coming from his men, which meant it might be time to try to get Sabrina to better cover. Shaw glanced at the front of the building.

So that Sabrina's pregnant belly wouldn't be smashed

against the ground, Shaw eased off her and moved her to a sitting position so that her back was against the brick wall. They were close. Too close. And face-to-face.

He found himself staring right into those sea-green eyes.

How will Shaw get Sabrina out?
Follow the daring rescue and the heartbreaking
aftermath in THE BABY'S GUARDIAN
by Delores Fossen,
available May 2010
from Harlequin Intrigue.

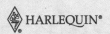

HARLEQUIN®

INTRIGUE®

BESTSELLING
HARLEQUIN INTRIGUE® AUTHOR

DELORES
FOSSEN

PRESENTS AN ALL-NEW
THRILLING TRILOGY

TEXAS MATERNITY:
HOSTAGES

When masked gunmen take over the maternity ward
at a San Antonio hospital, local cops, FBI and the scared
mothers can't figure out any possible motive. Before
long, secrets are revealed, and a city that has been on
edge since the siege began learns the truth behind the
negotiations and must deal with the fallout.

LOOK FOR

THE BABY'S GUARDIAN, *May*
DEVASTATING DADDY, *June*
THE MOMMY MYSTERY, *July*